KISS ME AT
Midnight

KISS ME AT

Midnight

A ROMANO FAMILY ROMANCE

LUCINDA WHITNEY

Lange House Press

Edited by Michele Holmes and Haley Swan
Cover design ©2018 Lange House Press
Layout and Formatting by LJP Creative
Published by Lange House Press

First Printing November 2018

ISBN-10: 1-944137-34-2
ISBN-13: 978-1-944137-34-2

Antes de tudo, somos família em nossos corações.

We are family first in our hearts.

Romano Family

- Francisco
  - *Mariana*
    - Tiago
    - Catarina
    - Daniel
    - André

- Luís
  - *Glória*
    - Matias

- Carlos
  - *Celestina*
    - Jacinta

António
Teresa

- Manuel
  - *Antónia*
    - Filipe
    - Luciana
    - Paulo
    - Ricardo

- Pedro
  - *Adelina*
    - Gabriela
    - Juliana
    - Alexandre

- José
  - *Patrícia*
    - Nuno
    - Susana

- Vicente
  - *Ana Maria*
    - Carlos
    - Pedro
    - Dinis
    - Anita

CHAPTER ONE

*P*ortugal. Home.

Filipe inhaled the scent of the ocean as he gazed into the dark-blue waters of the Atlantic. He dug his toes in the sand and his mind delved into the possibilities for his next project. The past four months away, volunteering in Angola drilling wells in remote villages, had been rewarding, but now he was ready for a different kind of challenge with the final stage of renovations of the hotel resort near the town of Peniche.

After a few minutes, he stood and carried his shoes in one hand. Once on the lawn, he brushed off the sand of and put on his socks and shoes, then cast another long look at the beach before turning to the building behind him. In the early morning, the crisp white façade of the five-story hotel lay in the shade. It would shine in the afternoon western light, and take on a golden hue as the sun set in the ocean.

1

The large swimming pool was empty at this hour and the parasols unopened. Even the blue lounge chairs, set in evenly spaced rows facing the pool, looked solitary without the guests that would soon come. To the right, the splash pool and children's park, under the partial shade of native pine trees and imported palms, cast a bright note against the dewy lawn.

Across from the hotel and on the side of the small road, the nine-hole golf course looked pristine and ready to be played. It wasn't the largest or the best in the country, but a serious contender against the others in the region. Filipe wasn't too worried, though; guests mainly came for the surfing and the beach. Anything else was an afterthought, however well planned.

He liked what he saw. Much had been done in the four months since his last visit, and the progress was on target for the grand reopening in a few weeks in early June. Now he just had to make sure all the details were up to his standards and that everything else was ready.

The walk from the front door of the hotel to the beach took between five and eight minutes, depending on one's speed and time of day. On the road that divided the front lawn and the flat banks preceding the sand, a wide crossing had been painted reflective white on the pavement to allow for the safe passage of pedestrians and golf carts. The cement path turned into smooth wooden slats that eventually disappeared into the soft sand.

He stood for a moment, watching the morning surf caress the shore in gentle waves. The air carried the crisp scent of sea and cold sand, and gulls above swooped down in noisy dives, looking for their breakfast. The beaches along the coast of Peniche were famed as some of the best in Portugal, at least where surfers were concerned. Tourists preferred the southern coastlines, with their clear waters and warm temperatures, but for surfing, the aficionados liked the wave variety, the flexible wind, and the overall rating of this beach. Since he'd be staying at the resort for a while, maybe he'd find the time for some early-morning surfing, weather permitting.

When the phone rang, Filipe reached in his pocket and pulled it out. After seeing the caller ID, he swiped at the screen. "I was just about to call you," he said in place of a greeting.

"Good morning to you too," Ross replied. "Did you arrive yet?"

"Just arrived in the past hour." Filipe started walking back.

"How was the trip?"

"It was amazing. I'll have to tell you all sometime," Filipe replied. "I'm taking a walk outside, and everything looks great."

"Was that you on the beach?" Ross asked.

Filipe stopped and raised his head to the hotel, squinting at the morning sun. "Where are you?"

"One of the suites at the top floor. The one where you'll be staying, actually," Ross said. "Do you want

3

to get together for breakfast before the meeting with the managers?"

"Yes, let's do that," Filipe replied. "Give me thirty minutes, and I'll meet you in the lobby."

After hanging up, Filipe approached the left side of the hotel, leading to the parking lot on the east. The guest spaces came first, followed by the staff area in the back. By the sidewalk, the newly painted handicapped slots close to the building awaited the signage, and at the far corner of the lot, five charging stations for electric cars stood equally spaced, an amenity that appealed to a lot of environment-conscious guests. In addition to these, the hotel boasted photovoltaic solar panels and a waste water reuse system, making the resort an icon of sustainability for its environmental protection and the use of renewable energies. Renovating an outdated hotel hadn't been as easy as building a new one, but the project had turned out just as he'd envisioned, if not better, and the marketing team predicted a profit by the second year. If it was wrong to feel proud of another sound investment, then let him be in the wrong.

An hour later, after a continental breakfast with Ross and a quick tour of the ground floor, Filipe was ready to assume his ownership. They moved to the board room on the second floor, which overlooked the swimming pool, the lawn, and, past the golf course, a stretch of beach that was visible through the trees and vegetation.

One by one, the managers and supervisors filled in the seats around the oblong table, curiosity and speculation in their expressions. Filipe sat to one side, observing them, bringing to mind what he'd learned from Ross about each person.

Ross Turner was his unofficial front man. Filipe had met him at an event in Lisbon a few years back, and after several mutual recommendations, Filipe had hired him. Having a Canadian father and a Portuguese mother, and being equally raised between the two countries, Ross was the perfect diplomat who knew the language and the customs of the land. When Filipe needed anonymity in a project, he sent Ross to be his public figure until he was ready to declare his involvement. The strategy had proved profitable on more than one occasion, as evidenced by the current one.

Ross took the front. "We've called this meeting to announce my role shifting to general manager as the new president takes his position at the SoliMar Resort."

A few eyes went wide, but no one said anything. Ross gestured to his right, and Filipe stood; then they switched positions.

"My name is Filipe Romano. As we get ready for the grand reopening, you'll see me in a more active role around the resort for the next few weeks. We have several points to go through this morning, so let's get started."

After introductions, Filipe opened his tablet and brought up the map of the resort and the surrounding areas on the flat screen hanging on the wall behind him.

"What did the surfing school say to our proposal?" Filipe asked.

"They're on board with cross promotion," the marketing manager replied and pulled up a new image on the screen. "We have a package that discounts bookings with them, and they're doing the same for us. Several bookings have already come in for the beginning of the surfing season."

The bookings manager added her report, and Filipe nodded, pleased with the numbers she presented.

"And the golf course?"

"The golf course is another amenity available to our guests and is also open to outside bookings, whenever the scheduling permits," the activities supervisor replied.

Filipe kept a list in front of him and checked off each item, adding a word of praise or thanks with his comments as the manager responsible for each department presented their update.

Having Ross leading the project from the beginning meant the employees had more connections and loyalty to Ross than Filipe, but that was a risk Filipe didn't mind taking since his schedule didn't let him be in all the right places at the right times. Delegating effectively was a sign of good leadership, as he'd learned himself.

"That brings us to the aquarium," he said, looking up from his tablet. "I noticed the outside walls and the building have received a coat of white paint to match the resort. What's the latest update on the sale?"

The small aquarium had been purchased by the last hotel owner, who'd had plans to expand it. It included a man-made freshwater pond, and it sat on a piece of property closer to the main road. Although not part of the resort, it could have been easily integrated if not for the ridiculous bureaucracy that made keeping up its licensing too much work. Filipe's financial advisers had urged him to sell to avoid future problems.

The sound of a voice clearing got Filipe's attention, and he turned to see a man in his early forties.

"The aquarium's director passed away six months ago," he said. "Since then, we've had difficulties that have prevented us from going ahead with the sale."

"And you are…," Filipe asked.

"I'm António Morais, the operations assistant manager," he replied. "The assistant director was unable to come." He fidgeted in his seat.

Filipe navigated to the map of the aquarium's interior. "How has this affected the guest visits?"

"We've been closed to guests for almost four months," he said.

Filipe frowned. "How does that affect the bottom line?"

"The former director had funds allocated to keep it going for six months. We have two months left of those."

"Funds allocated from where?" Filipe asked.

António Morais shrugged. "I'm not quite sure. You'll have to ask the assistant director, Alice Vieira."

It sounded like the aquarium might need a visit from him to find out what was really going on. Although included in the sale of the resort, it ran independently from the hotel, and it wouldn't interfere with the plans for the reopening week. But pleasing aesthetics were imperative, and with it being so close geographically, Filipe didn't want to leave anything to chance, especially when the financial situation wasn't immediately clear.

He and Ross wrapped up the meeting and thanked everyone for coming.

"Are you going over to see the aquarium?" Ross asked after the last person left.

Filipe nodded. "I need to find out what's happening there."

"Do you want me to come?"

"No, I'll handle it," Filipe replied. "You stay here and manage, Mr. General Manager," he added with a smirk.

Ross saluted him in reply. "Yes, sir."

Before something else came up that required his attention, Filipe pocketed his phone and set out to visit the aquarium.

Celeste exited the staff entrance and closed the door to the aquarium behind her. The sun beat high, already too warm for a May morning. Summer would be another scorcher, for sure. Maybe on Sunday afternoon she could take Lucas to the park in town. Her five-year-old was too serious at times, and she enjoyed playing with him outside.

The phone rang in Celeste's pocket, and she put down the bucket full of duck feed, then swiped at the screen.

Hugo. She groaned when she saw his name on the caller ID. Less and less, he had anything pleasant to say when he called. It couldn't be good news if he was calling today, just a few hours before he was supposed to take Lucas.

"Hugo," she answered, trying to keep her voice neutral.

"Olá, Celeste. How are you?" His smooth voice came over the speaker.

She closed her eyes and pinched her nose. And to think she used to love the sound of him. She'd fallen for Hugo Ferreira so fast and had brushed aside all the warning signs. How could she have had such lack of common sense and not seen him for what he was? "I'm fine. What's going on?"

"You always do that." His tone turned defensive. "Why do you always assume there's something going on when I call?"

"Because you never call unless you have an excuse to avoid doing your responsibilities." She'd learned that the hard way.

"Now you're just attacking me for no reason," he whined.

Celeste took a deep breath. "What can I do for you, Hugo?"

He sniffled. "Is Lucas around? I need to talk to him."

"I'm still at work." Where she usually was before lunchtime on weekdays, as he very well knew. "Lucas is at the daycare center. I can give him a message when I get home, or you can tell him yourself when you come to pick him up." Lucas spent every other Friday night and Saturday with his dad. At least, he was supposed to as defined in the custody agreement.

"About that," Hugo hedged. "My buddy Tony got tickets to watch The Kicks in a live concert in Lisbon. We're leaving this afternoon and won't be back until tomorrow night." He paused as if waiting for Celeste, but she held back from making a comment. "I won't be able to get Lucas this weekend. Will you tell him that?"

No, she didn't want to tell her little boy that his father had found something else to do on the weekend they were supposed to spend together. "I think it's best you call back at six and talk to him yourself. You haven't seen him in two weeks, and he misses you."

"I've been busy, Celeste. He knows that." He let out a long sigh. "Fine. I'll try to remember to call later."

Which meant he'd probably forget and she'd be the one to pass the excuse to Lucas. "Can you stop on your way out of town and give me the child support check?" It was a desperate effort on her part, hoping she could get the money from Hugo before he spent it.

"Something came up. I'll come by next week."

He hung up before she had a chance to reply.

Typical Hugo. He had money for a trip to Lisbon to watch a popular band but not enough to support his son.

If regret could kill. But no, she couldn't think that way. Despite all the pain Hugo had brought into her life, he'd also given her the best blessing, and she would never regret Lucas.

Celeste put the phone back into the apron pocket and retrieved the bucket, pushing the worry about Lucas's disappointment to the back of her mind. She'd deal with it later.

A movement caught her eye. Across the bridge, on the other side of the pond, the same dark-haired man she'd seen earlier was still walking around, taking notes on his phone and pausing every now and then to tug at his beard as if deep in thought. She'd seen him talk to António Morais, the operations assistant manager, which meant the man wasn't just a casual visitor poking his head in the closed aquarium. They did get curious people around from time to time, but they usually didn't make it past the gate.

She reached a hand in the bucket and absently threw the feed over the water. Some of the ducks rushed to the area, and she counted the old ones, making sure they were present, noticing the older swan still lagged behind his mate. She should have brought her lunch to eat on the bridge. Without visitors, Fridays were slow days that left her with too much time to wonder about should-have-beens, and that was the last thing she wanted.

Her thoughts turned to the mysterious man. Could he be a potential buyer? Or was he the aquarium's new owner already and nobody had told her?

Celeste wouldn't be surprised if Alice, the assistant director, knew about it and hadn't mentioned it, like last month when she'd forgotten to tell Celeste that Dr. Abarca was coming on Thursday instead of Tuesday. It hadn't been accidental in the least, of course. Luckily, Joana, one of the assistant keepers, had mentioned it in passing, and Celeste had been able to adjust the schedule to accommodate the temporary change. Another time, Alice had put Celeste on the weekend schedule, despite Celeste's request to the contrary. In the end, Heitor traded shifts with her, thank goodness.

Since the aquarium director's death six months ago, Alice had been acting more belligerent toward Celeste. Without Senhor Xavier's presence to act as a buffer between them, Alice continually let her true feelings come to the surface, making the work environment difficult for Celeste. Her coworkers commented on it, but what could she do? Did Alice want Celeste to quit? Alice's motivations weren't clear, a mix of jealousy and animosity that Celeste couldn't comprehend. Some days were definitely a challenge, no matter how much Celeste loved working at the aquarium.

The radio clipped to her belt crackled. "All personnel to the workroom, please," António said.

Celeste picked up the bucket, frowning. Personnel meetings always took place on Mondays. Why were they meeting so late in the week? With her curiosity piqued, Celeste hurried back to the building.

When she arrived, the other keepers were already there, as curious as she was.

"Did anyone see Alice today?" she asked.

They shook their heads. Nobody had seen her, which meant she had probably not come in. She'd done the same thing last Friday. It was true the aquarium didn't need as much personnel as when they'd been open to the public. Before his death, Senhor Xavier had sold off some of their larger exhibits and had reduced the personnel as a consequence, which had helped stretch their reduced budget. But the assistant director should still be present during the week—whether or not they had visitors.

Celeste tried to hide her annoyance at Alice's absence. As the head keeper, Celeste felt responsible for setting a good rapport with the other workers, and voicing her displeasure toward the assistant director didn't set the kind of example she wanted to have at the workplace.

The door swung open, and António entered the room, followed by the man she'd seen earlier. Behind the full beard, she couldn't tell the guy's expression too well. He was dressed casually, in jeans and a short-sleeve T-shirt that showed his defined biceps without too much effort. From his tanned skin, it appeared that he either worked out in a gym and spray tanned or maybe did some kind of manual labor outdoors. Either way, he was more attractive up close than from the glance she'd had of him earlier.

His brown eyes scanned the room slowly, and his mouth twitched. Maybe that was a smile? Hard to tell, with all that facial hair. When he caught her watching him, Celeste looked away, not wanting to give him the wrong impression. After Hugo, she was done with men.

"Is this it today?" António asked, not really needing a reply. He turned to the man and gestured to the personnel. "Looks like this is everyone today. We have one head keeper and four assistant keepers." He made quick introductions, and the guy nodded at each one of them, including her. "The assistant director is not available. Her name is Alice Vieira. I'm the operations assistant manager, as you know. The veterinarian, Dr. Abarca, comes on Tuesdays unless there's a problem. Everyone, this is Filipe Romano, the SoliMar's owner."

Celeste's breath caught, and her heart stopped for a beat. No, it couldn't be him. But how many Filipe Romanos could there be?

The last time she'd seen Filipe Romano he was nineteen, and he had certainly not looked like this man in front of her. This version was all grown up and mature, and she'd just been thinking of how attractive he was. Her face flushed, and her body went rigid. But it was him, now that she took a better look. The same nose and brow, same gorgeous, healthy hair. He'd always had such great hair. How had she not recognized him?

She became vaguely aware of everyone around her talking as he asked questions. And she was next. He was coming over to talk to her, and he had obviously not recognized her, unaware they knew each other.

"Excuse me," Celeste blurted, turning down the hallway. "I'll be right back," she said over her shoulder.

"Celeste, are you okay?" António asked.

She didn't stop to reply. When she arrived at the small bathroom, she locked the door with shaking fingers, then turned on the faucet and let the cold water run over the back of her hands as she tried to wrap her brain around seeing Filipe again.

All these years, she'd worked so hard at keeping the memories buried of what had happened that fated night. Everything had changed after that—her family had changed, she'd changed, her life had never been the same. So much pain and heartache.

What was Filipe Romano doing in Peniche? How was he the resort's owner? He could very well be. She didn't know anything about him anymore—what he did, how he earned his living. Twelve years was long enough for a man to come into his own with any kind of career—as he apparently had, being the new owner of a beach resort in one of the most popular areas in the country.

Celeste splashed her face with water, then turned off the faucet. She reached for a paper towel and patted her skin dry, inhaling deeply a couple of times, trying to slow down her rapid heart and uneven breathing. Her reflection caught her eye, and she grimaced—the unmade face, the hair falling out of the ponytail, the dirty apron over a worn T-shirt. It didn't matter. She didn't need to worry about making an impression, least of all on Filipe.

They were probably waiting for her return to talk about the aquarium or whatever he was here for. It would be expected of her as the head keeper to join the discussion.

Why couldn't she leave and keep pretending she'd never known Filipe Romano?

She walked back slowly, taking her time, putting off the inevitable for as long as she could. Back in the work room, Filipe stood at the front talking to her coworkers. She leaned against the wall, not knowing what to do or say. Her world had just flipped upside down and she was still trying to regain her footing. He glanced at her and frowned slightly, then returned his attention to the conversation.

A few minutes later, he wrapped up, and António called her over. "Celeste, I thought you could give Senhor Romano a tour of the tanks and grounds."

"Call me Filipe," he said.

The two men looked at her, and she averted her

eyes from Filipe, not ready to deal with his scrutiny of her. Had he recognized her at all?

"Sure," she replied. "Just follow me."

Behind her, Filipe said something to António. She didn't wait but turned out the door, anxious to be outside in the open, away from his presence so near her. All she needed was a good dose of fresh air and warm sun. And lots of distance between them. Then she'd be able to breathe and think and act normal again.

She could do this. She could give him a tour like the professional she was and go on with her life like he meant nothing to her. Because he didn't. He hadn't in a long time.

By the time he caught up, her breathing had slowed down, and her heart rate had regulated.

"Ready?" she asked in a bright voice. Maybe a little too bright.

"Celeste," he said in reply. "It's you, isn't it?"

CHAPTER TWO

$\mathcal{F}$ilipe hadn't been sure it was her at first.

When the operations assistant manager had introduced the aquarium's head keeper as Celeste Ferreira, Filipe had paused, as he usually did whenever he heard the name Celeste. His friend Celeste Quintano had meant so much to him that the name had always affected him strongly, even when he'd tried to forget how much it did.

This woman was blonde and curvier than the Celeste of his past, but hair color could easily be changed, and teenage girls eventually matured into adult women.

She'd left the room quickly just after he'd been introduced, and when she returned, he paid more attention to her, especially to the way she avoided looking at him.

But after António called her and she approached, he remembered her light-brown eyes.

How could he not have recognized those eyes immediately?

Of course she'd changed. Twelve years was a long time. She'd been seventeen, almost eighteen, the last time he'd seen her at her brother's funeral. She didn't even go by Quintano anymore, which meant she was married.

And the way she looked. The old attraction stirred inside him, the power of it taking him by surprise. After all this time and still so strong. At seventeen, she'd been pretty, but at twenty-nine she was gorgeous, even in a stained apron and old galoshes.

No, he couldn't think of her that way. She was completely off-limits for a long list of reasons, and especially now that she worked for him.

The guilt and shame of what he'd done so long ago crashed over him in a sudden wave, as fresh and raw as if it had happened yesterday instead of all those years ago. Heat filled his chest and crept up his neck, and the oppression of it stole his breath for a brief moment.

Filipe fisted his hands then released his fingers, willing it all way. The regret had lived with him for so long until it had become part of him, inevitable and inescapable, just something else he couldn't change about himself like the color of his eyes. He'd learned to cope with until it became bearable, and now, with one look at her, it was all back.

How could he ever atone for what he'd done? How could she ever forgive him?

She finally looked at him straight on. "Yes, it's me." Her face remained impassive and expressionless with no hint whatsoever that anything had bothered her. Maybe it didn't matter to her anymore as much as it mattered to him.

"You've changed," he said lamely.

"So have you," she retorted. "The beard."

Filipe passed a hand over his facial hair. "I just arrived from a trip this morning. It's not usually this long. You're blonde now."

Her hair had been a lighter shade of brown, with even brighter highlights in the summer, but it was a lot lighter now.

"What kind of questions do you have? About the aquarium," she added.

That's what he was there for, to find out more about the aquarium. There could never be anything personal between them. As awkward as the situation was, he was the boss. Celeste was employed here, and the purchase of the resort had included the aquarium.

And she was still his best friend's little sister, even if Eduardo had passed away in a motorcycle accident. She'd been off-limits before and was even more so now.

It still made sense to sell the aquarium, as the financial analysts had advised, and he'd known the sale would affect the aquarium's employees, but now it felt more personal. Someone who'd meant a great deal to him at one point in his life worked here. What

21

would she do if she lost this job? How would that affect her family? How many children did she have, and what did her husband do?

But he didn't have a right to ask any questions. Not personal ones.

"How many people work here full time?" he asked.

She stopped under the shade of a tree, careful to stay at arm's length. "Alice is not here today. She's the assistant director. You've met António, the operations assistant manager. I'm the head keeper, and Marco, Heitor, Luís, and Joana are the assistant keepers you just met. Senhor Taveira is the only one left from the janitorial staff, and Pascoal is the groundskeeper. A lot of other employees arranged transfers when Senhor Xavier announced the downsizing, and since the closing to visitors there hasn't been a need for more staff."

Filipe nodded. It made sense, of course. The fewer animals in the exhibits, the less work all around.

He followed her around the grounds, to the pond and aviary enclosure, and listened to her as she talked about the birds, which were mostly ducks, geese, and swans who shared the pond waters with small decorative fish of various sizes and colors. Filipe and Celeste crossed the bridge, then made their way back to the main building.

She walked ahead and unlocked the double doors, then held one open for him, not even giving him the chance to do it for her. Was it to emphasize her employee status, to make sure he didn't forget he was there to talk business? As if he could muster the courage to mention anything else.

The building opened to a wide room with two-story-high ceilings, with a small gift shop to the right, which was now closed. In the center, a wide, waist-high enclosure full of water contained smaller fish, small stingrays, and other aquatic animals.

She gestured towards it. "That's our salt water petting pool. It was very popular with children. We'll come back to it on the way out."

Filipe nodded.

"This is the way to the large exhibits," Celeste said as she walked down a hallway.

As they emerged, the echo of her voice reverberated off the tanks, some empty and some full.

"The three seals were the first to go to a zoo in southern Spain." Celeste kept walking. "We still have a few small penguins and a couple of otters."

The room passed into a hallway leading to the reptile exhibits. Celeste kept talking about the animals they still had at the aquarium. He half listened to her, half thought about the times he and Celeste and Eduardo had spent together. The three of them had been practically inseparable at one time.

Celeste and Eduardo were only fifteen months apart in age. They moved into the neighborhood one summer and Filipe met them when he and Eduardo were in tenth grade and Celeste in ninth. Filipe was close to this cousins Matias and Tiago, but he mainly saw them for school breaks and summer vacations.

Gaining friends that lived so close had been a high point for Filipe.

Life had been so simple back then, so much easier.

"So you're the new owner," Celeste said, bringing him back to the present.

He nodded.

"Are you going to sell the aquarium?"

"That was the plan. The main focus has always been the renovation of the hotel and resort. I was away for a while, and I'd expected it to be sold already."

"Well, you can't sell without a renewed license, and you can't get a license until you pass the inspection," Celeste said. "We've been in bureaucratic limbo for months. You'll have to talk to Alice. I know there have been some problems with licensing after we flunked the first inspection. Senhor Xavier had been working on it, but that's all I know." She paused and glanced at him. "Is there any chance you'll change your mind?"

"About what?"

They exited the main building and stood outside in the afternoon shine. He was desperate for something to ground him, something to focus on and lead him away from the crazy memories about Celeste swirling around in his head. A breeze from the ocean ruffled the foliage on the trees, and the scent calmed Filipe.

"About selling the aquarium," Celeste replied. "It wasn't always like this. With some investment and dedication, it could be brought back. In any case, we'll need to pass the inspection to get the new license. After that, we could open the aquarium to visitors and school trips again." Her voice was hopeful and her expression expectant.

The location had a lot of charm, and he could almost imagine how it must have been at its best. "It doesn't really fit with the plans for the resort." The newly painted walls were only a cosmetic fix, temporary and barely scratching the surface. From what he'd seen on the tour, the aquarium needed major renovations.

"No, it doesn't fit with the resort." Celeste squared her shoulders, and her face hardened. "It was never meant to. The aquarium was built first. The hotel came a decade later." She reached behind her back and untied her apron, then balled it in her hands. "Do you have any other questions?"

"Actually, I wanted to ask if—" He stopped as he watched her walk back to the employee building, not waiting for him.

That probably meant no more questions for now.

Filipe rubbed the back of his neck and blew out a long breath.

He couldn't blame her for leaving. It had been too great of a shock for both of them, meeting like this.

But there was nothing he could do about it—he was her boss, and she was off-limits. He'd repeat that in his mind until he knew it by heart.

Celeste hung the broom behind the kitchen door and looked around. She'd spent her Saturday morning cleaning and doing laundry, as she usually did every Saturday, and she was finally done. The feeling of accomplishment flashed for a moment. As small as it was, she would enjoy it while it lasted. She approached the open window and leaned on the sill, letting her thoughts catch up with her.

The two-bedroom apartment was tiny but adequate for her and Lucas. To the front, there was a galley kitchen, and a combination dining/living room with a balcony spanned the width; the bathroom and a closet stood in the middle, with two bedrooms to the back. It was as modest as the two-story building from the nineties, in a village barely large enough to be called such. Renting in Peniche, the closest town, was out of the question since, it had become too expensive after being discovered as a prime surfing location.

After lunch, a run to the store was long overdue. She'd planned to go on Friday after work, but with Hugo's phone call and the shock of meeting Filipe, the rest of her day had completely derailed.

The night hadn't gone much better, with anxiety keeping her awake for half of it. By the time she rose from bed in the early morning, she'd resigned herself into accepting there wasn't much she could do about the situations with either man: Hugo was not likely to change his ways anytime soon, since he'd never done it in the eight years she'd known him, and Filipe owned the aquarium where she worked, whether she liked it or not.

What she could do was to keep taking care of the animals and fish at work and be the best parent she could. Being a good mother did not fill the place of an absent father, but she would do everything in her power to make up for the difference.

Celeste blew out an impatient breath as a slight breeze blew her hair back from her face. She pulled away from the window. Enough with the pity party. It never led anywhere.

She found Lucas on his bedroom floor, playing with toy cars. Sometimes he was so quiet, she almost forgot to check on him while she did the housework. Lucas would start first grade in September, and she feared he wasn't socially ready for it.

"Are you ready for lunch?" She sat on the floor next to him, legs crossed.

He didn't reply right away. It always broke her heart to see Lucas so downcast after Hugo canceled on him. How could the man not see what he was missing? He had a son who loved spending time with him, and he didn't care about it.

"How about we go to the park after the grocery store?" she asked.

"Can we do something else?" he asked, still pushing the car on the rug, back and forth.

Hugo usually took him to the park, so maybe Lucas didn't want to be reminded of that.

"Sure. What do you have in mind?"

He paused and raised his eyes to her. "Can we feed the swans?"

Celeste smiled at him. "That's a great idea. I'm sure they'll love to see you."

Lucas's little face brightened, and, for a moment, it was a small victory that she'd engaged his attention and had him looking forward to doing something he liked.

She fixed a quick lunch for them, then packed the reusable shopping bags and set out to Peniche with Lucas in the back seat, praying the whole time the old car wouldn't break down. When they arrived, the store was full, and it took longer to shop with her list of coupons and items on sale than what she was used to. Lucas hung on to the side of the cart, and Celeste tried to be efficient and patient as they made slow progress at the checkout lane.

When they arrived at the aquarium, she parked under a tree and used her keys to unlock the employee entrance. It spoke of Lucas's sweet, quiet character that of all the animals he could visit he liked to feed the swans the best.

She retrieved a small bucket from the workroom, then found the bag of feed she kept on hand for such occasions and filled the bucket halfway. Lucas came forward and took it from her, grabbing it with both hands.

Heitor, who worked on weekends, exited the main building and greeted them. "My favorite duck feeder is back," he said in his bright Brazilian accent, putting up his palm for Lucas. "Tudo bem, Lucas?" Heitor had emigrated from the São Paulo area over ten years ago, but his accent remained untainted.

"Tudo bem, Heitor," Lucas replied in his best Brazilian accent as part of their usual exchange. He set down the bucket and high-fived Heitor. "I'm feeding the swans, Heitor, not the ducks," he said, dropping the accent. "You know that."

Heitor frowned deeply and rubbed his chin, almost comical in the intensity of his expression. "Are you sure the swans are the only ones that come to eat?"

Lucas's expression bloomed in a wide smile. "I sure hope not," he replied enthusiastically. He always looked forward to seeing all the birds, not just the swans.

Heitor laughed. "Good luck, young man."

"Goodbye, old man," Lucas said, not missing a beat, still smiling as Heitor left with a wink.

Celeste watched, a hand over her chest, wishing she could bring Lucas to the aquarium every day, hoping he could be the carefree boy he was here all the time and everywhere else. But that wouldn't be realistic. It was the wish of a mother's heart, to see her child happy and unburdened. Despite his young age, Lucas worried. But here, at the aquarium, he let free of those worries and acted more like the five-year-old she knew he was.

They set out walking toward the pond. "Do you need help?" she asked.

"I can do it, Mamã. You keep forgetting I'm a big boy now," he said seriously. That was his reply to almost everything since his fifth birthday.

Celeste suppressed a smile. "You're right. I keep forgetting that." He was growing too fast and she was not ready for it. One of these days he'd drop the Mamã and would start calling her Mãe. There was nothing wrong with being called Mother, but it would hurt a little for what it represented.

When they arrived, Lucas walked to his favorite spot and set down the bucket. He placed his hands around his mouth and called aloud. "Here, Flip! Here, Bete!"

It amazed her to see the swans responding to a little boy's voice, gliding through the pond until they stopped in front of Lucas, the ducks and geese following behind and the fish bobbing near the surface.

Lucas laughed out loud and turned to her. "Did you see that, Mamã? They remember me."

"They do, don't they?"

He brought a finger to his chin. "Why is Flip so slow today?" He'd noticed it too.

"I'm not sure. I'll have Dr. Abarca take a look on Tuesday." The old swan had been eating less and getting slower lately.

Celeste picked up the bucket and dumped it inside the raised bowl at the edge of the pond. With their long necks, the swans easily reached the food, then turned to the water surface and shared with the fish who'd congregated around them.

Lucas clapped. "They are sharing, mamã!"

That was Lucas's favorite part of feeding the swans, the way the birds fed the fish.

At the sound of steps behind them, Celeste turned to see who approached.

Filipe.

Something inside her stomach coiled, an emotion she couldn't describe and could barely remember, as he walked toward her and Lucas. He'd trimmed his long beard to a stylish scruff that showed off the angle of his jawline and his high cheek bones, even the shape of his mouth. This face was more familiar than the one she'd seen yesterday. He almost looked like the old Filipe she remembered, only more developed and mature and much more attractive than the memories she had. And his full lips. Why couldn't she have forgotten the memories she had of those?

"Olá," Lucas said. He'd turned to see the stranger as well, curiosity shining in his eyes.

"Olá," Filipe replied. He nodded at Celeste, and she nodded back. "Mind if I join you? I came to see what you're doing." He looked from Lucas to her, and she could see all the questions in his gaze.

Lucas's coloring was darker than hers as he physically resembled his father. Something she had a hard time with.

"Who are you?" Lucas asked.

Celeste resisted the urge to take Lucas's hand. "He's the aquarium's owner."

At this, Lucas took a step forward, obviously interested. "You are? You own the whole thing?"

"He owns the whole thing," Celeste replied.

Filipe shrugged, as if owning the aquarium was something he didn't have any control over. He paused at the edge of the pond, not very far from them.

Lucas wasn't fazed. "My name is Lucas Eduardo Ferreira, and this is my mom. People call her Celeste. What's your name?"

If Filipe had doubts about Lucas's identity, he didn't anymore. She looked down at Lucas, entirely surprised at his friendliness.

"Hi, Lucas. Hi, Celeste." He went down on his heels and addressed Lucas, extending his hand. "My name is Filipe. I actually knew your mother a long time ago."

"You did?" Lucas looked up at her, and she nodded. "And your name is Filipe?" He took Filipe's hand and gave it one good shake up and down before releasing it quickly. "Guess what? The male swan's name is Filipe too." He pointed at the swans. "But I call him Flip. That's his wife, Bete. Her real name is Elizabete. Do you also have a wife named Elizabete?"

Celeste cringed. "Lucas, we don't ask questions like that." She glanced at Filipe. "I'm sorry. He's not usually like this." Was this her shy son who never talked to strangers?

"Why not?" Lucas frowned.

"He's okay," Filipe interrupted, making eye contact with her, a soft expression on his face. "I don't mind the questions. No, I don't have a wife named Elizabete."

"What's your wife's name?"

Goodness, he had so many questions today. Unwilling, her own curiosity surfaced. What was the name of Filipe's wife?

"I don't have a wife." Filipe flicked his eyes in her direction, so quick she almost missed it. "How do you know which is the male and which one is the female?" Filipe asked, settling comfortably beside Lucas.

"That's easy, silly. The male is the tall one. Do you know why their names are Filipe and Elizabete? Because they're named after the Queen of England and her husband. These swans came from England. But they understand Portuguese now." Lucas said in a matter-of-fact tone. "I know a lot about swans." His little chest puffed up.

"I don't know anything about swans," Filipe said. "What can you tell me?"

Lucas tilted his head. "Believe it or not, swans can sleep on land or water."

"Really?" Filipe asked. "What else do you know?"

"Believe it or not, swans can fly," Lucas continued in the same tone, parroting one of his favorite television programs about animals and nature.

"Where did you learn so much about swans?" Filipe asked.

"I like to watch educational shows," Lucas replied. "And we get books from the library and my mom reads to me."

"You're a very smart boy, Lucas."

"Yes, I know," Lucas said confidently, and Celeste chuckled. "My mom says so all the time." Lucas beamed at her, and she smiled back.

In a few minutes, he'd talked more with a stranger than he had talked all week. Why? Was Filipe like this with all children? Or did he have more personal experience in dealing with kids? Maybe he didn't have a wife now, but he could have been married at one time and have children of his own.

Lucas kept talking with Filipe. Celeste hung back, watching them. At a glance, Lucas would more easily pass as Filipe's son than he would hers.

The thought stopped her as her gaze rested on the two figures, Filipe sitting on the ground next to Lucas, their coloring so similar.

"So what's your favorite thing about swans?" Filipe asked.

"Believe it or not, swans mate for life," Lucas replied, his voice almost reverent. "Do you know what that means?"

"What does it mean?" Filipe lowered his voice to match Lucas's.

"It means that when a male swan and a female swan get married, they stay together for their whole lives."

"Why do you like that?"

Celeste held her breath for a moment, waiting for Lucas's reply. When had he paid attention to the mating habits of swans? He was only five.

"I like that because it means that swans don't get divorced and baby swans can have a mom and a dad with them all the time."

She stood, shaken by the words. From the corner of her eye, she felt Filipe's gaze on her, which she avoided at all costs. She would not look at him.

"Lucas," she said, purposefully calming her voice. "Should we get going? We need to put the groceries away and get started on dinner."

He straightened his small frame. "Is it pizza night?"

"Yes, it's pizza night," she replied, her jumbled emotions beginning to slow down.

Lucas threw his arms in the air. "Yay, pizza night." Then he turned to Filipe. "Come with us, Filipe. My mom makes the best pizza."

Her heart jumped in her chest. She looked to Filipe, who'd stood from his spot near the edge of the pond and already watched her with an unreadable expression.

He walked to Lucas and crouched in front of him. "I really appreciate the invitation, Lucas, but today's not a good day."

"Tomorrow?"

"Tomorrow I'm going to Porto to see my family. Maybe some other time, okay?" Filipe stood.

"Okay," Lucas replied. He picked up the empty bucket and waved at the swans. "Xau, Flip. Xau, Bete. Xau, Filipe," he added.

"Xau, Lucas. It was nice meeting you," Filipe said.

Celeste gave Filipe some version of a neutral smile, not knowing what to say or do, then trailed behind her son.

As emotionally hard as yesterday's meeting with Filipe had been, today's encounter could only be described as bizarre, what with the friendly exchange between Lucas and him.

And thanks to Lucas's comments about swans mating for life, Filipe could very well guess her family situation.

Somehow, she had a feeling there was more to come.

CHAPTER THREE

$\mathcal{F}$ilipe leaned against the wall and observed the large room from his corner. After talking to Mom on the phone on Friday night, she'd insisted he come to Porto for a visit. And when Mom asked, he knew better than to argue with her, even if the visit didn't come at a convenient time.

Now, as he watched his crazy family, he was glad to have made the drive. Luciana wasn't there, of course, as she was in New York with her boyfriend, and his younger brothers, Paulo and Ricardo, were away at college and hadn't been able to come on short notice. Some of the cousins had come, and a feeling of nostalgia sneaked up on him, as it usually did when they got together and caught up. It didn't bring back the old times like before, but it filled part of the emptiness in that one corner of his heart. He was good at ignoring that part of him, the part that had threatened to take over after Eduardo's death. The constant projects, long hours, and new challenges all helped. But...

With Matias and Vanessa's wedding coming up soon, a lot of the preparations were in full swing to get ready for such a large event. Despite Vanessa's family being in charge of the reception, the Romanos wouldn't let the occasion go by without a celebratory get-together.

Filipe didn't know a thing about planning a wedding, but he'd heard a few comments tonight about how much stress it could put on a couple. Looking at Matias and Vanessa, he knew they were okay, even better than okay. Their love for each other was written in their expressions, in the way they treated each other.

For the first time in a long while, Filipe felt something inside him, a little jab of an emotion. Was that jealousy, wishing he could have the same thing his cousin did? Wishing for that kind of happiness with someone else who'd want to have it with him?

Unbidden, Celeste invaded his thoughts. He couldn't stop thinking about her; hadn't been able to since they'd met at the aquarium on Friday. After having banned her from his brain for more than a decade, it felt strange that she occupied so much space in such a short time.

Meeting her again on Saturday had been completely unplanned. He'd been at the aquarium to take some notes, but when he'd seen her walk by with a child, he'd followed before he'd given himself a chance to let his common sense kick in. Apparently, he didn't have any good sense at all where Celeste was concerned, just like when he'd been a teenager. Some things never changed.

At first, he wasn't sure if the child was hers. The boy didn't particularly look like her, which, of course, didn't mean he wasn't her son. Lucas probably took after his father, who must be the one with the strong dark genes. Filipe had thought for sure she was married, but the boy's talk about the swans and divorce hadn't left any doubts about his mother's status. Divorce wasn't something a five-year-old talked about unless he had experience with it.

What kind of father was Celeste's ex-husband? What kind of husband had he been?

And why was Filipe so curious? Celeste's family situation and marital status were none of his business. They'd been friends a long time ago, and there was nothing else between them anymore. Now she was his employee, and Filipe would do well to remember that.

When Tia Mariana and Jacinta approached Vanessa, Matias kissed his fiancée on the cheek and walked over to Filipe.

"It's good to have you back. How was the trip to Angola?" Matias settled on a chair and Filipe took the other next to him.

"It was both intense and inspirational. The people are so poor, and it's incredible to see how something we take for granted makes such a difference in their lives."

"What were you doing exactly?"

"I traveled with a clean water initiative that drills wells in villages." He told Matias about his experiences in the Southern African villages. "I was supposed to go for six weeks and ended up staying for four months. I would have stayed longer, but the resort is getting ready to open, and I need to be here for that."

"Another project of yours coming to an end. Are you throwing a big party when it opens?"

Filipe shrugged. "Not too big. A press conference for the ribbon cutting, plus cocktails with a VIP guest list. You know how it is." Networking wasn't always his favorite thing to do, but Filipe had learned that meeting the right people and cultivating business connections usually paid off at some time.

"I'll have to bring Vanessa for a visit soon," Matias said. "She could use the time off." His tone was wary.

"Are things not going well?"

"She's been kind of stressed with the wedding preparations. Her grandparents are throwing the party of the year, sparing no expense. I can understand their thinking, but Vanessa wasn't raised like that, and she's having a hard time with it. I'll be happy when it's all over, to tell you the truth."

Filipe nodded. "I can imagine. Planning high society events is not easy." Although he wasn't at the same financial level as the Valadares fortune, he'd been doing well enough to have some experience with those types of gatherings.

"Be glad your project is going well and you don't have to deal with the headaches of pleasing everyone's tastes."

Filipe didn't reply. Everything was going well at the resort, but he was still coming to terms with seeing Celeste.

At his lack of reply, Matias turned to him. "You're too quiet, primo. What's going on you're not telling me? Having regrets about the investment?"

Filipe rubbed his chin. "Regrets, yes, but not the kind you're thinking. The resort was a sound investment, and I'm glad I took the chance with it. Did you know the purchase included a small aquarium?"

"That sounds fun," Matias said.

"Not really. It's been closed to visitors for a few months. The director passed away, and after that, the place didn't pass inspection. Now they're missing some of the exhibits, the personnel is cut in half, and I still haven't met the assistant director, who's supposed to tell me what's going on."

"But?" Matias prompted.

"I met most of the other employees on Friday, including the head keeper, or aquarist, like they call them. And I'm still reeling from it."

Matias chuckled lightly. "That bad, huh?"

"Do you remember that one summer all the cousins spent together at Grandma and Grandpa's farm?" At Matias's nod, Filipe kept going. "Do you remember how I brought my friends to spend two weeks there?"

"The brother and sister?"

"Yeah, Eduardo and Celeste."

"I remember how close the three of you were. Wasn't there a family tragedy a few years later?"

"Eduardo died in a motorcycle crash." Filipe sighed. "I was young and stupid, and I didn't know how to deal with Eduardo's death. I left after the funeral and never had contact with the family again."

"That's understandable. Shock and grief can really mess a person up." He glanced at Filipe. "I sense there's more to the story."

"I met Celeste on Friday. She's the head keeper at the aquarium."

Matias's eyebrows shot up. "What are the chances after all these years?"

Filipe nodded. "I know, right?"

"And now you're her boss."

"I am, but not directly. She works for me, but she answers to the aquarium's assistant director." Ultimately, Filipe was the assistant director's boss, but for now he didn't intend to introduce any changes in the chain of command, unless it became necessary.

"What did she say when she saw you there?"

"I think she was just as shocked as I was. She even left the room." Looking back, he realized she'd been visibly shaken. "I went back to the aquarium yesterday and met her five-year-old son. At first I thought she was married, but her son let it slip that his parents are divorced." He frowned. "What five-year-old knows what divorce means unless he's been affected by it?"

Matias nodded. "That's sad. Poor kid. But it makes sense. How is her family doing?"

Filipe shook his head. "I have no idea. We didn't talk about anything personal, and I'm not even sure she would welcome it. Everything was strictly business."

"Well, you didn't ask for my advice, but I'm going to offer it anyway," Matias said. "Take it or leave it. It's up to you."

Matias's background in the tourism industry as a river cruise captain had him leaning toward diplomacy a bit too much at times. "Spit it out already," Filipe said.

"Not everyone has a shot at a second chance."

Filipe waited for more but nothing else came. He frowned. "That's it? I have a shot at a second chance?"

"You need to ask yourself, do I want this chance? Or will I regret it if I don't take it?" Matias stood with a smile on his face. Filipe followed to see the cause of his cousin's attention as Vanessa met Matias halfway and he leaned in to kiss her on the lips. Then he dropped an arm around her waist and brought her close to his side.

Filipe watched the happy couple for a few minutes, love and contentment practically oozing from them. As much as he wanted to pretend he didn't envy that kind of relationship, he couldn't deny the little pang of longing deep in his chest.

Had Matias just given him an object lesson for a secure, loving relationship?

Celeste looked out the glass double doors, tossed wide open to welcome the warm spring day. Across the lobby in the office, Filipe and Alice sat around the small desk. Filipe had arrived earlier to meet with Alice and go over the records of the last year the aquarium was open. Alice had started on the other side of desk, and every time she stood, she moved closer to Filipe.

How did he not see what a snake that woman was? Alice always had an ulterior motive for her actions, and Celeste had the perfect words to describe the assistant director—shrewd and calculating.

Celeste would have liked to sit in on that conversation, but she hadn't been invited and she had work to do. It was much better that she didn't get involved anyway.

For some reason, Alice didn't like Celeste, and Celeste hadn't been able to figure out why. Alice had kept her animosity under wraps when Senhor Xavier was still alive, but after his death it seemed she didn't feel the need to contain it. Fortunately for Celeste, Alice didn't like to get dirty, and Celeste's job included plenty of manual work that was far from clean. Working with animals never was—like today, scrubbing the frog tanks. She refilled her water bottle and walked back to the amphibian exhibit.

Celeste's mind strayed to the plans she'd made for the inspection. Without a new license, the aquarium couldn't be sold, and opening to the public was out of the question for the time being. Would Filipe really go ahead with the sale? How long would that take to set up? What if nobody was interested in taking over a struggling aquarium? Then they'd have to sell the rest of the animals first and the building and property separately. What about everyone's jobs? What would she do if she lost her job?

She sighed as she loaded environmentally safe detergent onto the brush. The aquarium had been part of her life even before she'd gone to college. She had volunteered there for two summers and still had one semester to finish when Senhor Xavier asked if she was interested in the assistant aquarist position. One of the aquarists had left for a better job, and the director had difficulties filling the position. But Celeste had been perfect for it since she could take a lower pay as she didn't have her degree yet.

A year later, when the head aquarist left to assume a much-coveted position at the oceanarium in Lisbon, Senhor Xavier promoted Celeste. By then, she was pregnant and didn't complete the semester she needed to graduate. Her pregnancy had been the catalyst for a lot of changes in her life, starting with the shotgun wedding between her and Hugo. At the time, she'd been convinced it was the best decision. After all, they'd been in love, and the baby deserved a mother and father to raise him together. Hugo had readily proposed and promised her she'd be able to finish her studies after the baby was born.

But that hadn't happened. So many of his promises and her plans had never come to fruition. Looking back, it was easy to see how skewed her judgment had been, being pregnant and hormonal and having a smooth-talking boyfriend-soon-turned-husband who was agreeable and helpful.

That hadn't lasted too long at all.

If it wasn't for the aquarium's budget, she probably wouldn't have the job, and if she had to start over somewhere else, she'd never manage to get the same kind of pay she had here. Not to mention her housing situation. Renting a small apartment in Atouguia was within her means, and she liked it there—close enough to work and the beach. What more could she ask for?

So many worries.

Could Filipe be convinced to postpone the sale? If she showed him the plans she had to reopen the aquarium, would he consider it? As much as she didn't want to ask him, he was the man who could change the outcome.

The Filipe she knew when they were younger would have done what he could to help. The new Filipe, she didn't know. She could only hope he'd be open to new ideas and suggestions.

Celeste kept working until lunchtime. She had an apple and a sandwich waiting for her in the refrigerator, and she'd have to go and get it later. For now, she sat under the shade of a tree for a few minutes of rest. The day was warm and the sky clear, the kind of day where Lucas would love to be outside feeding the swans. Was he having a good day? She worried about him, about how his days went at daycare, whether he had little friends or not. And next year he'd be going to public school, and she well remembered how cruel kids could be when they felt like it.

Across the pond, Filipe exited the main building, walking purposefully toward the gate. While he stopped to examine it, Celeste stood from her spot and crossed the bridge. This was her chance to talk to him about her plans, if he was willing to listen. It was Wednesday already, and she'd been building her courage to approach him all week. Today was the day.

"Filipe, do you have a few minutes?"

He stepped away from the gate and turned to look at her. "Hi, Celeste. What can I do for you?"

His expression was friendly and open, as if he had a smile ready to shine on her. She remembered well those smiles, the way his eyes crinkled in a happy manner at the sight of her. Her heart had always skipped a beat, like it did just now. Traitorous heart.

She'd planned exactly what to say before, but now, standing this close to him, her brain failed her. "I. . .huh." How embarrassing.

Celeste crossed her arms and looked away for brief moment, scraping the toe of her work shoe on the hot pavement.

Filipe's eyebrows furrowed lightly, but he didn't say anything.

"I've been working on two different plans for the aquarium, one short term and one long, and I'd like to show them to you." This time the words came out too fast. Her cheeks heated, and she brought a hand over her chin, partially hiding her mouth.

"You know I'm going ahead with the sale, right?"

Was holding out hope that she could change his mind completely dumb and useless? Or was it worth the risk?

"You still need to get the license renewed."

"Yes, I do." He nodded slowly. "Where do you want to talk?"

Her eyes widened. "Right now?" She hadn't expected him to be this receptive.

He pulled out his phone from his pocket. "Did you eat lunch yet?"

"No, not yet."

"Do you have an hour for lunch break?" he asked. When she nodded, his shoulders relaxed a little. "We can eat at the restaurant and talk about getting the license back. If that's okay with you," he added.

Was that insecurity in his voice or just disinterest? Whatever it was, she didn't care. Sitting down to share a meal with him, at the hotel he owned, no less, hadn't been in her plans, but she'd take it if that meant she could have his attention for a few minutes.

"Yeah, that's fine." She ran her hands along the sides of her apron. One thing was sure—she couldn't go into his fancy hotel restaurant looking like this. "Why don't you go on ahead, and I'll catch up with you. I need to get the papers from my locker."

He gave her a long look, taking in her appearance, and his eyes danced with light amusement. She wanted to open her mouth and tell him she wouldn't be changing for him or because of him. While that was true, mentioning it would only bring more attention to her appearance, and that was the last thing she wanted.

Fifteen minutes later, she entered the hotel lobby with a legal folder in her hand. She'd changed into a buttoned shirt she kept in her locker for last-minute meetings, and she'd combed her hair. At least her jeans were clean. As she looked around, Filipe pulled away from the check-in desk and walked toward her.

The lobby charmed with understated elegance and quiet comfort. It was decorated in white and dark blue with yellow accents for a decidedly marine theme that brought the beach inside. Everything evoked the ocean, from the colors to the decorations to the murals. Even the air fresheners carried the tangy scent of a low tide. As casual and relaxed as it looked, someone had paid an interior designer a lot of money for such a job well done. Filipe, of course. He was the new owner, after all.

When he reached her, he lifted his hand as if to touch her on the shoulder but then let it drop. Celeste tensed immediately, anticipating the contact. In the end, she was both relieved and disappointed, and mad at herself for wishing he had done it instead of pulling away at the last minute.

"This way," he said, holding a door open for her. "We'll be eating on the patio."

She followed him through a large empty dining room with a wall of glass doors that opened to a patio facing the beach. Round tables with open umbrellas for shade dotted the area. The view was spectacular, and Celeste found herself unable to look away from the expanse before them.

Filipe pulled out a chair for her, then sat across.

"I take it you like it," he said with a hint of a smile.

Celeste dragged her eyes away from the panorama and concentrated on him. "Like what?"

"The view, for starters. Maybe the hotel." He didn't say it as a question, but the implication was there. Did he seek her approval?

"From the little I saw, it looks amazing. But you already know that."

A waiter interrupted them to hand them menus and take their drink orders.

"I hope you don't mind the restricted menu," Filipe said. "The chef and the kitchen staff are in trial mode until we open. After next week, we'll have everything available."

There was one choice for meat and one for fish. Celeste ordered the fish of the day, and Filipe chose the same. A few minutes later, the waiter returned with their salads. The menu had a decidedly traditional inspiration, with lighter ingredients suitable for the younger generation that most likely made the bulk of the market Filipe targeted.

When the entrées arrived, Celeste held back from eating too fast so she could jump into her plans.

"The food is delicious. Thank you," she said.

"You're welcome. How long have you been working at the aquarium?"

"A little over six years. I started as a volunteer and was hired when a full-time position opened. And you? How did you get into real estate?" She was eager to pull the subject of the conversation away from her.

"I started in construction, first as a day laborer and soon as a shift manager, later on as a general contractor. Once I had the experience and contacts, I jumped to flipping houses and condo buildings. After a couple of good investments, I was able to expand, and the rest is history." He shrugged, as if such a career success weren't a big deal.

"So you never did architecture at the University of Porto?" Filipe and Eduardo, her brother, had talked about going together.

"No. After—" He winced and looked away.

Celeste resisted the urge to stand and leave. She was not ready to talk about what had happened the night of Eduardo's accident. Not yet. But it was inevitable. Now that Filipe was back in her life, even if just as her employer, she would confront him. Reopening old wounds was never easy, and she needed to build up her courage and get some closure.

Before she could react, Filipe pushed his plate away and reached for her folder. The mood between them had gone from easy and light to heavy and dark. She'd do well to remember they weren't friends like before. He was the owner and would be selling the place where she worked. Unless she could change his mind.

"Your research is impressive," he said at last, leaning back on the chair. "I'll be honest. I didn't know what to expect, but this three-stage plan clearly shows you've done your homework."

Even though he most likely meant it as a compliment, it almost bordered on insulting. She brushed the feeling away. "I am a professional, you know. And I have experience in the field. I'm good for more than cleaning tanks."

"I don't doubt it." He watched her for a long moment, his focused attention unsettling her. "What did you study in college?"

"Marine biology." If it came up, she'd admit she hadn't finished the last semester, but since he hadn't asked, she didn't feel the need to offer the information.

The way he looked at her unnerved her. What was he thinking?

"Okay, let's do it."

"You'll do it? Which one of the plans?" A surge of hope rose in her chest.

"Let's get the aquarium in top shape. Any improvements we do will make it easier to sell."

Something inside her deflated. Of course he was thinking like a businessman. She was the one who had more than a professional interest in the place. For him, it was business as usual. The opportunity and potential to change his mind were still there, though, and she'd be foolish to say no on account of his motives.

Celeste squared her shoulders and extended her hand. "Let's shake on it."

For a brief moment, Filipe hesitated. Then he took her hand in his and shook it.

At the contact, a spark of energy jolted up her arm, and the small hairs at the nape of her neck stood on end. The memories rushed through her, the way they'd touched and kissed the night before he left. She removed her hand from his, maybe a little faster than good manners suggested, anxious to put some distance between them.

Touching him wasn't a good idea. Not a good idea at all.

CHAPTER FOUR

$\mathcal{C}$eleste glanced at the screen of her phone one more time. It was Hugo's weekend with Lucas, and he hadn't come yet. He hadn't called either. If she didn't leave in five minutes, she would be late to work.

Heitor had called her late on Friday night to ask her to take his shift today on account of a family emergency. Of course, Alice had been unreachable as she usually was. Everybody else had to work on the weekend at some point, but Alice always managed to evade that.

After trying Hugo's number one more time without a reply, Celeste went to Lucas's bedroom and grabbed his backpack. "Come on, Lucas, you're coming with Mamã today."

Lucas appeared at the door as she packed some essentials for the day. Daycare was closed on Saturdays, and she hadn't set up a babysitter because Hugo should have picked him up.

Celeste sighed. She should have known better. Hugo couldn't be counted on.

"Are you mad at me, Mamã?" He looked at her with a frown between his eyebrows.

She paused to look at him with a smile. "Of course not, Lucas. You're coming with me to the aquarium, and you'll have lots of fun. You can pet the stingrays and we can feed the swans again."

His expression was hesitant, and her heart went to him. Celeste knelt in front of him. "I'm sorry your dad wasn't able to come get you. Why don't you choose one book and one toy to put in your backpack?"

He nodded, a little shadow of a smile making a brief appearance.

On the way to the aquarium, Celeste silently cursed the day she'd met Hugo Ferreira. Charismatic, charming Hugo who'd turned into undependable, unsteady Hugo. Next time he called, she wouldn't answer. He didn't deserve to be the father to such a special child as Lucas.

When they passed through the gate, Lucas's mood improved. He ran on ahead, and she followed him as he veered toward the pond. She had work to do inside first, and he wouldn't like that.

"Hey, you're here too," Lucas exclaimed. "How did you get here before we did?"

"Hi there, buddy. How are you?"

Celeste stopped and turned her gaze toward the deep male voice. Of course Filipe would be here. It shouldn't surprise her to see him working on the weekends now that they had a firm plan for the renovations and improvements.

Filipe walked toward Lucas and held his hand up in greeting.

Without missing a beat, Lucas stretched and slammed his much smaller hand against Filipe's.

"Did you forget my name? It's Lucas, not buddy."

"You are so right. Sorry, Lucas. You've come to feed the swans?"

"My mom needs to work today, and my dad forgot to pick me up, so I came with her. If I behave, my mom will take me for ice cream before we go home."

Celeste's eyes widened, caught by surprise at Lucas's chattiness and candor. Reluctantly, she approached Filipe. "I'm sorry I had to bring him with me. He does behave well, and I'll keep him out of the way."

"He's fine." Filipe winked at Lucas. "Don't worry about it. You're not usually on the schedule for Saturday, are you?"

"Heitor had an emergency, and he asked me to cover. I should be done by lunchtime."

Lucas reached inside the feeder and tossed the leftover pellets at the fish.

"What is it that you'll be doing today?" he asked.

"Feeding and diet preparation."

"What does that entail?"

She rushed to explain. "Cutting up food in the galley and making sure each animal and fish gets what it needs." It involved a little more than that, but she didn't need to elaborate.

He nodded.

"And you?" she asked, gesturing at the paper in his hand. "What are you doing today?"

Filipe folded the paper and slipped it into his pocket. "Just double-checking some measurements."

A little chuckle came from the side, and they both turned to see Lucas leaning over the edge of the pond. Celeste's heart jumped in her chest. He was too close to the water.

Before she had the time to move, Filipe reached Lucas in two long strides and gently pulled him back. "Have you been to the beach lately, Lucas?" he asked.

As her heart rate returned to a normal beat, Celeste came closer, chiding herself for her distraction.

"My mamã doesn't like to go to the beach when it's cold," Lucas replied.

Filipe's mouth hitched in a small smile. "I don't think it'll be cold at all today." He pinned a gaze on her, and she guessed what he wanted to ask.

Memories rushed back of that last summer, when they'd been able to communicate with just a look between them. They'd been so close back then, always in tune with each other. Celeste shook the impression, then nodded back at Filipe, giving him permission.

"Would you like to come to the beach with me?" He asked Lucas. "I need to make sure the sand is clean for next week."

Lucas turned his face to Filipe first, then to Celeste. "Can I go with Filipe to the beach, Mamã? I promise I'll be good."

Filipe caught her eye, and Celeste found herself wishing she could go too.

The thought surprised her. Why was she thinking of spending even more time with Filipe? She'd already told herself what a bad idea it was; she knew it was.

She headed toward the building, and they followed her, Lucas between them, skipping along.

"What's next week?" Lucas asked.

"You see the hotel over there?" Filipe gestured toward it. "It's finally ready to reopen, so I'm having a party for the employees on Thursday."

Lucas tipped his chin up to look at Filipe. "A party? Can I come? And Mamã too? I'm not old enough to go places by myself."

Filipe chuckled. "No, I suppose you're not."

"Lucas, it's not good manners to invite yourself," Celeste said. "You wait until somebody invites you."

Filipe turned to her. "He's invited, and so are you." He then addressed Lucas. "I hope to see you and your mamã there. Will you come?"

Lucas grinned and grabbed her hand. "Mamã, Filipe invited us. Can I say yes?"

"You can tell Filipe we'll come."

"We're coming," Lucas replied with too much enthusiasm.

When they reached the main employee building, the three of them stood by the door.

Celeste retrieved Lucas's backpack and placed it on his shoulders. "He's got some things to keep him entertained, plus snacks, a water bottle, a hat, and sunscreen." She told Filipe but kept her eye contact on Lucas, bending down to kiss his forehead. "You be a good boy, all right? And don't forget to put your sunscreen on."

When Filipe turned his palm toward Lucas, Lucas took it without hesitation. Her breath caught, surprise filling her at how easily Lucas trusted Filipe, how fast he'd become friends with the man she'd loved as a teenager.

They turned to go, and Lucas waved at her. "Xau, Mamã."

"Filipe," she called after them. "Can I have your cell number?"

She caught up to them and palmed her phone, then brought up the screen for new contacts.

"Sorry, I didn't even think about it."

They exchanged numbers, then Filipe left with Lucas as before, hand in hand.

"Don't feel obligated to watch him the whole time," she said. "Bring him back in an hour. Or sooner, if you want to."

Filipe gave her a thumbs up and Lucas imitated him.

Celeste smiled; she couldn't help it. Lucas was so cute, even if she was biased. And Filipe—well, he was unexpected.

Then, before her mind took off with comparisons between Filipe and Hugo, she walked to the main building and slipped on her apron. In the office, she retrieved the diet sheets and observation records, the food inventory, and the charge slips. She switched to her favorite soft rock station on her phone and placed it in the wide glass cup that sat on the shelf, then went through each list, making note as she read.

The fresh fruits and vegetables had been delivered on Friday, and the freezer held the meats and fish already portioned, which had been done immediately after delivery. In the pantry, she retrieved the dietary supplements and dry pellet food.

For the next hour, Celeste diced, chopped, and mashed food and supplements and then placed them in the appropriate labeled bins. Some would be frozen for the feedings on Sunday and Monday, and some she would deliver to the animals and fish today. Heitor was resuming his normal schedule on Sunday, and he would finish the tasks she'd started today. Marco, the other assistant aquarist, had already begun the cleaning, evidenced by the missing cart with all the supplies. They'd probably meet at some point in the course of the morning.

Working alone, without interruptions or distractions, Celeste breezed through her tasks, appreciating the time alone. The tension she'd been accumulating all week slowly seeped out, and she let her mind wander. As she walked through the aquarium, feeding and taking notes, talking and interacting with the animals and fish she knew so well, she felt part of her balance restored. She loved it here. How could she even entertain starting over somewhere else?

But how could she convince Filipe to turn his mind from his plan of selling the aquarium?

Thoughts of Filipe brought Lucas to mind, plus a twinge of guilt at having forgotten him for a brief time. Celeste pulled out her phone from her pocket and noticed a missed text message.

I took Lucas to lunch. We'll be back soon.

She frowned. Was she a crazy, unfit mother for sending her five-year-old son with a man she hadn't seen in so many years? It was true that Filipe and she had been close friends, but that was in the past. She didn't know what he'd been doing in the twelve years since then. A surge of motherly panic flashed through her.

The time stamp on the text read thirty minutes earlier, and they might have been on their way already. If they took much longer, she'd go looking for them.

As Celeste returned the cart she'd been using to be refilled with the next batch of food, the happy sounds of Lucas's chatter accompanied by a deep male voice reached her ears. They were back, and she went to meet them at the door.

Lucas placed his arms around her waist and hugged her quickly. "Mamã, it was so much fun! Filipe and me walked all of the beach and we picked up shells and special rocks. And then he took me to the big building and I saw a magazine full of swans."

Relief washed through her. Lucas was fine. Nothing bad had happened. Maybe Filipe wasn't the same nineteen-year-old she'd known, but he wasn't someone to fear. Her neck heated for the way she'd doubted him for a moment.

Lucas went on, describing the day in great detail, and absently dropped his backpack on the floor.

Filipe picked it up and handed it to her.

"Lucas, say thank you," she told him, as he continued chatting without paying attention to what she'd said.

Filipe chuckled lightly. "He might crash at some point today, but I don't think he's there yet."

"He'll get there after dinner, I hope," Celeste said, still watching her son and the energy he carried.

"Dinner?" Lucas asked. Of course, that was the one word he zeroed in on. "Is Filipe coming to dinner with us? Yay!" He jumped up and down for a few seconds, as if the idea of having Filipe over was the best part of his day.

Filipe put out a hand on Lucas's shoulder. "I think your mom might have—"

"Will you come?" she interrupted. "If you're not busy." Her neck heated at the way she blurted the words out.

What was she doing? One minute she was suspecting him of taking off with her son and the next inviting him over for dinner with her and Lucas.

Filipe lifted a brow. "No, I'm not busy tonight."

"Come over at seven."

His eyes softened. "I will." Was that a smile tugging at the corner of his mouth? Why

He said goodbye to Lucas and then left.

"Why is your face all red, Mamã?"

She touched her cheek. "Is it?"

Filipe climbed the stairs to the second floor and stopped in front of Celeste's apartment door. He inhaled deeply and let it out slowly. Where did these jitters come from?

The handles on the bags dug into his fingers, and he shifted the weight. He'd been thinking about Celeste and Lucas all day. Spending time with Lucas had been a delight, especially their visit to the beach, where they'd collected small shells and the occasional sea-polished stone or piece of glass.

Lucas had insisted on it after Filipe told him how he and his mom had picked shells and stones when they were younger. They hadn't been little kids by then, already in tenth and ninth grade, but the search had taken on the same earnestness, at least for him. Celeste had been fixated on collecting natural heart-shaped rocks, and Filipe had joined her when Eduardo wasn't around.

From Lucas's reaction, it wasn't likely she still collected them or even had her collection around.

He raised his hand and rapped on the door.

From inside, Lucas's voice yelled, "I'll get it!" and his hurried steps followed.

The door opened but stopped short with the chain. Lucas peeked out and grinned. "You came."

"Olá, Lucas. Can you tell your mom I'm here?"

"She's coming. I can't reach the chain."

His eyes fell on the bags. "What do you have there?"

"A surprise and ice cream for dessert."

Lucas turned around. "Mamã, Filipe has ice cream."

A minute later, the door closed and the chain rattled, then the door opened again.

Celeste swung it wide. "Sorry it took me so long. I was getting a dish out of the oven."

As soon as Filipe entered the apartment, Lucas took the bag with the ice cream from his hands and ran down the short hallway. Filipe set the other bag on the narrow credenza by the front door.

"Come on," Celeste said, walking ahead of him. "We're eating in the kitchen. Lucas, did you put the ice cream in the freezer?"

When she and Filipe entered the kitchen, Lucas had a guilty expression on his face and his hands behind his back. Filipe felt a laugh coming to the surface, but Celeste's stern face put a quick stop to it.

"Lucas Eduardo Ferreira, did you open the container? Where is it?"

"I put it in the freezer, Mamã. It was getting all melty."

Celeste's expression softened. The ice cream was not the only one getting all melty. It was hard to resist that little face, and Filipe wasn't even the parent.

She sent Lucas to the bathroom to wash his face and hands, then grabbed the olive oil and vinegar to sprinkle them on the salad before tossing it.

Filipe observed mother and son, and something twinged in his chest. The relationship these two had touched him in a way he didn't want to think about, but his mind and heart had different plans.

What would have happened if Eduardo hadn't died? Would Filipe and Celeste have had a chance at making it together? Maybe they would have married, and they'd have two or three kids by now, even one who was five and liked to dip a spoon in the ice cream before dinner.

He shoved the thought away as far as he could. That would never be. The guilt he carried for his part in Eduardo's death ensured nothing could ever happen between him and Celeste. It was better this way.

The meal passed quickly. She'd baked a lasagna in the oven, and it reminded him of Avó Teresa's recipe. Sitting directly across from Celeste, he had the perfect view of her face and her reactions to him and Lucas. In his years in business, Filipe had cultivated the talent of reading body language of those with whom he interacted. To her son, Celeste was open and giving; but to him, she had a cautious guard subtly emanating from her, walls raised and determined to not let him in unless he proved himself trustworthy.

Filipe couldn't blame her.

Lucas, who knew his fair share of kindergarten jokes, provided the entertainment. When his repertoire ran out, he proceeded to tell his mom a detailed account of their earlier trip to the beach.

"And then Filipe gave me a plastic bucket and we picked up shells, Mamã."

"I know, amor. You showed them to me, remember?"

She called him love, and Filipe didn't doubt how much she loved him.

"We found some smooth rocks, but none that were heart shaped."

Celeste paused with her fork in midair, and her eyes rose to Filipe's. "You told him?"

Filipe shrugged. "I thought you still had your collection and he'd have seen it by now." But Lucas hadn't known what Filipe was taking about when he learned of his mother's obsession with heart-shaped rocks.

Celeste patted Lucas's hand and a small smile lifted the corner of her mouth. "I used to have a few heart-shaped rocks, but I kind of lost them a long time ago. We can start a new collection, if you want."

At the suggestion, Lucas brightened. "We can go to the beach every day and get more."

"Probably not every day, but I like your idea of getting new ones."

"You'll help us find heart-shaped rocks, won't you, Filipe?"

"Sure.," Filipe nodded. He found himself unable to deny Lucas his enthusiasm for rock collecting.

The ringing of a phone interrupted them, and Celeste swiped at the screen then frowned. She hesitated for a fraction of a second. "Excuse me. I need to take this."

As soon as his mom left the kitchen, Lucas pushed his plate away from him. "I'm done. Can we have dessert now?"

Filipe peered at the plate. "Do you think your mom would want you to finish your salad greens before dessert?" He didn't have any kids of his own, but he remembered how his mom had constantly pushed him and his siblings to eat all sorts of greens. Popular opinion said that moms were the same everywhere in the world, so Filipe figured he was safe in his assumptions.

By the time Celeste returned, Lucas had finished his salad and Filipe had served him dessert, then started washing the dishes.

Celeste took a seat and drained her glass of water. "I'm sorry. I didn't mean to be gone that long." Her tension was back, heavy in her tight shoulders and weary frown.

Filipe rinsed the plate in his hands and set it on the drying rack. "Lucas, I left a bag on the table by the front door. Why don't you go see what it is?"

"Can I be excused, Mamã?" At his mom's nod, Lucas jumped from his chair and left.

Celeste's shoulders relaxed a little, as if she could get a reprieve while her son was away. Did she ever get a break from her responsibilities?

Filipe eyed the tea kettle sitting on the stove, filled it with cold water, and lighted a burner to put it on. "Teacups?"

Celeste pointed at the cabinet, and he drew out one small plate and matching cup. The sugar container sat on the counter, between the flour and the salt, and he placed it on the table.

"Tea bags?"

"In the other cabinet," she replied.

When the water boiled and the kettle whistled, Filipe turned off the burner. He placed a bag of lemon-balm tea in the cup and poured the water over it.

"The spoons are in that drawer." Celeste jutted her chin in its direction, and Filipe retrieved a spoon.

It was June and maybe a tad too warm for sipping tea, but Celeste needed something to help her calm down.

"How did you know?" she asked.

"I remembered." So many little things he knew about Celeste were slowly resurfacing.

For a moment neither of them talked as she stirred a spoonful of sugar in the amber liquid in concentric motions.

"What's in the bag?" Celeste asked, breaking the silence.

"What bag?"

"The one you sent Lucas for."

He'd forgotten about it. "It's a photo book with marine animals."

A pale smile graced her lips. "No wonder he didn't come back." She took a drink and looked at him over the brim of her cup. "Thank you. Lucas will love it." Another slow sip. "You didn't have to."

Filipe kept stirring. "I saw it online when I was looking for something else and thought of him."

"That's kind of you. Thank you again for taking Lucas this morning and sacrificing your time."

"It wasn't a sacrifice. I enjoyed it," Filipe said with a faraway look. "He's an amazing kid, and you've done a great job with him."

She evaded his eyes and a blush flushed her cheeks. Did she think differently? Did she not know what he said was true? Did she even have anyone in her life who supported and encouraged her?

Instead of commenting, she gestured at the sink. "I didn't invite you over to do my dinner dishes."

Filipe shrugged. His dad and grandpa had always said, if there was work that needed to be done, why not do it? He believed it, and he always preferred to keep his hands busy, anyway.

After a pause he asked, "Is everything okay?"

"As okay as can be expected, I guess," she said after another long sip.

Filipe waited. As curious as he was, he wouldn't push her for more.

"It's about my dad," she said at last. "He's back in rehab and asking to see me."

"Where is he?"

"In Matosinhos, at the Alberto Silva Clinic."

The clinic specialized in alcoholism rehabilitation and was located a few kilometers outside of Porto. He'd sent a donation in the past.

"And your mom?"

Celeste rubbed a spot on the side of her neck. "My mom passed away a year after Eduardo. Almost to the day."

Filipe hid his shock. Her mother and brother were gone, and her father, even though he was alive, was not in a position to offer the kind of family support she needed.

His family wasn't perfect, but he knew he could always count on them for whatever came up. The same went for his extended family, and the closeness he had with his cousins brought him the same kind of comfort his sister and brothers did. He had both parents and grandparents and aunts and uncles, and all of them had an interest in his life. He couldn't imagine his life without all of them.

And what did Celeste have? An alcoholic father and an ex-husband who didn't show up to pick up his own kid.

How did she do it? Where did she get the strength?

The admiration for her burned in his chest. "You're a strong woman, Celeste."

After staring at the cup in her hands, she said, "I wish it were true."

What could he say that would help her see what he saw? He hardly had the words that would make a difference.

Shame pricked at him for not being there for her in the past twelve years. He'd left like a coward in the still of the night, unable to face his mistakes and confess his guilt to her. Instead of staying and being her friend, Filipe had effectively blocked her out of his life.

Maybe it was too late to have the kind of relationship he used to want with her, but there must be other ways he could help.

Without pausing to think, he grabbed her free hand and held it in his. "I know I wasn't there after Eduardo—when you needed me. I'm sorry. I know I've given you no reason to trust me, but I hope you'll let me be a friend when you need one."

Celeste held his gaze, and something zinged between them. His skin burned at the contact with hers, and surprise flashed in her eyes. The old chemistry between them was still there, very much alive and kicking. She'd felt it too.

This could be a problem.

Lucas entered the kitchen with the open book in his hands, and Celeste quickly dropped her fingers from his. She straightened in her chair and extended a hand to Lucas.

"What do you have there, sweetie?" She added a bright smile to her words.

"It's a book about sea animals." Lucas turned to Filipe. "Is this your book?"

"No, it's yours," Filipe said with a smile.

Lucas dropped the book on the table and threw his little arms around Filipe's neck and squeezed. "Obrigado! This is the best day ever!"

Filipe choked back the emotion in his throat. Something as simple as a book had made the little guy so happy. What if Filipe could be a part of their lives? Even a little bit?

They moved from the kitchen to the living room, where Lucas insisted the three of them sit on the sofa, with him in the middle. They spent some time poring over the book as Lucas showed his favorite photos to Celeste and Filipe,while they took turns reading the captions to him.

It warmed Filipe's heart to see Lucas so happy.

Thirty minutes later, Lucas started yawning.

"It's time for bed, Lucas," Celeste said. "Go change into your pajamas and brush your teeth, please." She stood from the sofa. "And say goodbye to Filipe."

Filipe rose. That was his cue. "I should be going. It's getting late."

Lucas crossed his arms and pouted. "I don't want to go to bed. I'm not tired." He struggled to hide another yawn, and Filipe and Celeste chuckled.

Celeste pulled the book from his lap. "It's way past your bedtime, silly boy. Go get ready and I'll read you a story."

Lucas stood and latched on to Filipe's leg, then tipped his head back to look up at him. "Can you read me a bedtime story, Filipe? Please?"

Celeste placed a hand on Lucas's shoulders. "Honey—"

"I'll make a deal with you," Filipe said, meeting the boy's gaze. "You go do what your mom asked, and I'll come read one story to you."

Filipe put his hand out, and Lucas jumped up to hit it. "Deal!" He disappeared down the hallway.

Celeste brought a hand to her forehead and sighed. "I'm sorry. He's just starved for male attention, so to have you here..." She let her words trail off.

Filipe touched her upper arm. "I don't mind, Celeste. I truly don't."

The story didn't take too long, as Lucas fell asleep midway through it. Filipe pulled the sheets up on Lucas's sleeping form and smoothed the hair on his brow, thinking about the ifs in his life—if only he had gone with Eduardo that night, if only he'd stayed all those years ago...

When Filipe returned to the living room, Celeste moved from the window and approached him. "Thank you," she said in a low voice.

Automatically, Filipe bridged the distance between them and opened his arms, feeling like a fool for the three seconds that passed before Celeste surprised him, leaning into his embrace, her hands resting on his chest.

He held his breath and wrapped his arms around her back, hardly believing what was happening. The embrace was light, but the glorious feeling of having her back in his arms almost undid him.

He loved her. After all these years, Filipe still loved Celeste.

CHAPTER FIVE

$\mathcal{F}$ilipe walked to the cooler in the shade and got a water bottle, then took a long swig. He waved good-bye to the contractor and the laborers he'd brought in yesterday, who'd be around for at least two weeks, or as long as needed. The short-term goal was to get the aquarium ready to pass the inspection first and go from there with the rest of the renovation to facilitate the sale.

Monday had been a very busy day and so had today. Working alongside the other men made him feel right at home with the physical labor. This was the kind of work he knew well, the work he'd started in when he'd left home. Early on he'd learned that working hard until he was tired proved to be the best way to deal with problems.

Yesterday and today he'd had only a glimpse of Celeste here and there as she went about her tasks, and the longing to talk to her and be closer to her grew inside him more and more.

He missed Celeste. He missed Lucas too.

The time he'd spent with both of them on Saturday had only helped strengthen his feelings. Realizing he was still in love with Celeste had surprised him. It was like the love he felt for her had been dormant, just waiting for them to find each other again, and now that they had, it seemed different and more intense. And he couldn't get her out of his mind.

Filipe gave himself a mental shake. This was why he kept busy with work. Getting distracted with feelings and dreams was too easy and led to a place he wasn't ready to deal with.

Grabbing an empty bucket, he walked around the grounds and picked up any garbage that had been left behind during the day, sorting out the plastics and occasional glass to be placed in the recycling bins.

At the sound of loud honking and squawking, Filipe paused. Celeste stood in the shallow end of the pond, wearing rubber galoshes nearly up to her hips. She had one of the swans pinned under her left arm while the other flapped its wings too close for comfort. Geese and ducks swam nearby, noisily protesting at whatever was going on.

Filipe placed the bucket on the ground and walked over to Celeste in slow, measured steps, not wanting to aggravate the situation.

"Do you need some help, Celeste?" He kept his voice low, hoping she could hear him.

She remained in the same spot, holding on to the swan's body with one hand and cradling his beak in the other. "I got a good grip on his mandible and humeri, but I lost my momentum to get out of the water."

"Excuse me?" he said in reply.

"I got his wings and beak. Now I just need to get myself out."

He took a step closer. "What if I come behind you and grab your elbow?"

Celeste inhaled. "Let's try that, but no sudden movements, please. I don't want to lose this guy and have to start over."

Filipe inched his way toward Celeste and gripped her arm above the elbow. Using his weight as an anchor, she stepped out of the pond onto the firm ground, and Filipe followed her.

"Will the other swan come after this one?" he asked.

"She'll stay." Celeste looked briefly over her shoulder. "She doesn't like it, but she'll stay."

"What's going on?"

"This guy hasn't been feeling well, and I need to put him in quarantine. The vet is coming to take a look."

Filipe walked on ahead of her and opened the doors to the building. Once in the quarantine pens, Celeste set the swan inside a pen that had been prepared for its arrival. She backed away slowly and locked the gate, then let out a deep sigh. "I can breathe again. Thanks for the help. You came at the right time."

"Do you manhandle swans by yourself a lot?"

Celeste chuckled. "Not when I can help it. Heitor or Luís are usually on hand for assistance, but I didn't know we'd need to move this guy today. Dr. Abarca called and said he can swing by after all, but he's on a tight schedule and asked to have Flip out of the pond."

"Is that his name for real?"

"Did you think Lucas made it up?" She pinned him with a pointed look, eyebrow raised.

He had thought that, actually. "In my defense, Lucas is only five."

"Maybe he's only five, but he knows everything about the swans. And that includes their names." Celeste grabbed a clipboard and wrote some notes.

"Are you still going to see your father on Saturday?"

She glanced at him, then went back to her notes. "I'm planning to leave early."

"My cousin Matias is getting married in Porto on Saturday, and I'm driving up. There's plenty of room for you and Lucas." He winced inside. Not the smoothest invitation.

"I haven't decided what I'm doing yet. Can I get back with you?"

"Sure." After watching Celeste, Filipe searched for ways to bring up their growing friendship, but he caught himself in time. "Do you mind if I stick around? I haven't met the veterinarian yet."

She replaced the clipboard on to its hook and looked up at him. "Of course not. You own the place."

Her tone was matter-of-fact, but he couldn't help but wonder what she really meant underneath her cool exterior.

"A place I know nothing about," he replied.

"Tell me when you want to know more, and I'm your—" Her cheeks turned scarlet.

What had she been about to say?

"I meant to say I'm the right person for the job. But not the only person. There are others—"

Filipe raised a hand. If she weren't embarrassed and trying so hard to fix what she'd said, he'd have told her how cute she was all flustered. But that wouldn't be appropriate. "Don't worry about it. I know what you meant. For the record, I'd rather learn about the aquarium from you than anyone else."

Another blush rose to her cheeks. She watched him intently, and, for a moment, her eyes strayed to his lips.

Filipe's chest heated and he took a step toward her. "Listen, what happened on—"

Celeste's phone rang, and she quickly stepped away from him. She glanced at the screen. "It's Dr. Abarca. I better go let him in."

Filipe rubbed the back of his neck and let out a deep sigh. He'd almost crossed the line with Celeste at work. It was one thing to have dinner at her place and play with her son; another thing was getting too close at work where he was the owner and she the head keeper.

At the sound of chatter and laughter, he relaxed his shoulders and tried to look casual. When Celeste entered with the vet, Filipe stared. Dr. Abarca was nothing like he'd expected. Young, tall, and walking too closely to Celeste. The two of them smiled like they were good friends. Maybe even very good friends. A surge of irritation pricked Filipe.

Dr. Abarca extended his hand. "I'm Nuno Abarca. How are you?"

"Filipe Romano." He shook his hand. Firm grip, eye contact, a definite sizing up after flicking his gaze to Celeste. Had Celeste told the good doctor about their friendship?

Nuno Abarca set a large bag on the cement floor and bent over it. "I'm glad you're renovating the aquarium. It's about time, if you ask me."

Celeste shrugged at Filipe but didn't correct the veterinarian.

When Dr. Abarca and Celeste entered the pen where the swan was and started conferring about the bird's health, Filipe excused himself.

"It was nice meeting you, Dr. Abarca." Not really. "Celeste, I'll see you tomorrow."

She looked over her shoulder and smiled at him. "Thanks again for your help."

The irritation followed him as he walked back to the hotel. Only it wasn't irritation, if he was being honest. Jealousy would be more accurate.

Filipe had brought a contractor with a small team of laborers on Monday to start the renovations at the aquarium. He was there every day working alongside them, consulting with Celeste at least once during the day, even when he really didn't need to. In truth, she shouldn't have been surprised at his work ethic. He'd always been a hard worker.

Alice hadn't come right out and said anything about the way Filipe deferred to the aquarist instead of the assistant director, but her displeasure was evident to Celeste. Around Filipe, Alice kept her mood in check and her opinions to herself, and that was a calculated move, as Celeste knew.

After the embrace Celeste had shared with Filipe on Saturday night, she feared the tension between them would escalate and put a stop to their tentative friendship. On Tuesday, they'd almost had a moment by the quarantine pen. She'd seen it in his gaze, the intent to kiss her. But Dr. Abarca had arrived and interrupted, thank goodness.

After that, Filipe had treated her as if nothing had happened between them, and her disappointment was almost more than she wanted to admit, even to herself. It had felt so natural to go to him when he opened his arms in her living room. She still remembered the hug they had shared at Eduardo's funeral—warm, safe, like being where she was supposed to be and nowhere else mattered.

On the other hand, maybe it was better this way. He'd made a brief mention about not being there but hadn't offered an explanation of why he'd left so abruptly all those years ago, and deep down, she feared placing her trust on him. Without knowing what to expect from him, the risk was too great, and her track record wasn't exactly the best—she'd also trusted Hugo in the beginning, and that hadn't turned out well at all. How could she trust her judgment now?

She'd told Filipe she'd think about riding with him to Porto, even though she already knew what she wanted to do. Not necessarily the same as what she needed to do.

Today, Filipe had held a meeting with everyone that worked at the aquarium to share the renovation schedule for the next few weeks. Unfortunately, instead of asking Alice about the employees' shifts, he'd asked Celeste again. Alice's hostile expression would come back to haunt her, and Celeste was not looking forward to that.

Later in the day, Alice approached Celeste near the otter enclosure. Celeste had spent the last two hours observing the old swan, writing down her notes to share with the other keepers and with Dr. Abarca at his next visit.

Alice crossed her arms and leaned against the wall. "I left the employee files on your desk."

Celeste paused her note-taking. "What for?"

"The quarterly performance evaluation. For everyone, including yourself."

Celeste frowned. "They're not due for another six weeks."

"It's for the new owner. I'll need those in the morning." Alice turned to leave.

"Wait a minute," Celeste called after her. "There's thirty minutes left before I clock out. How do you propose I finish those evaluations? I won't have time."

"You can add overtime to your hours today. Just have the evaluations on my desk before I arrive in the morning." She left, her heels clacking on the cement floor.

Celeste stood, watching Alice leave, dumbfounded at the exchange. She pulled her cell phone from her pocket—twenty minutes until six.

Lucas. How was she supposed to pick him up from daycare at six thirty, like she did every day?

Hugo wouldn't reply to a last-minute request, not in the middle of the week. She knew by now how unreliable he was.

When she arrived at her desk, the stack of folders was there, as Alice had said. She was supposed to cross-reference each person's schedule and their daily performed tasks for the last three months. She'd done it before but not at the end of the day to be turned in the next morning.

Celeste sighed and sat down, then scrolled through her contacts again, although she already knew the answer. She really didn't have anyone who could get Lucas and watch him for a couple of hours until she finished the job.

A text popped up, and she swiped at the screen. **How is that swan doing?**

Filipe.

Just under observation for now. Thanks again for the help.

No problem, he replied.

You left really quickly yesterday.

Didn't want to be in the way. Are you almost done for the day?

She hesitated, not wanting to tell him how Alice had created extra work for her at the last minute.

Something came up, and I have to stay late. Any chance you could pick up Lucas? I'm sorry I'm asking with such short notice, but I hadn't planned on staying.

The phone rang with a call from Filipe, and Celeste answered.

"You don't need to apologize, Celeste. Of course I'll get Lucas. Is he at day care?"

Relief and gratitude filled her chest, and her shoulders relaxed with tension she hadn't even noticed.

"Thank you. You have no idea how helpful you are." She sat back against the chair. "Yes, Lucas is at daycare and he needs to be picked up by six thirty."

"In Peniche?"

"No, in Atouguia, not far from my apartment." Celeste gave him directions. "I'm going to call the daycare and tell them you're coming so they'll release Lucas to you."

"Do you want me to bring him to the hotel?"

She glanced at the folders. At least two hours' worth of work, if not three. "Would you be okay with taking him to the apartment if I give you my keys?"

"Good thinking. That way I can put him to bed on time."

"Yes, that would be great. I owe you a big one."

"Don't even say that. You don't owe me anything. I'll be right there to get your keys."

Celeste stood and made her way to the gate, where she could meet Filipe before he came in and asked questions about the work she had to do.

Why wasn't he married? He was attractive, well-off financially, trustworthy, and hardworking. He even liked little kids. Didn't other women see what a great catch he was? Was there a problem she didn't know about? Did he not pick up his socks, or did he snore too loud? And what did those matter when he had so many good qualities going for him?

When Filipe arrived, he seemed excited about spending time with Lucas, as if it wasn't really doing her a favor at all but the other way around.

He handed a paper bag to her.

"What's this?"

"Dinner. You probably don't have any since you weren't planning on staying."

Maybe he wasn't as distracted as she'd believed him to be. Hugo would never have thought of bringing something for her. "You're right. I don't have anything to eat. Thank you."

He was thoughtful and mindful too.

She told him about the vegetable soup in the refrigerator, and he promised to give Lucas a balanced dinner, then took the keys and left with a smile on his face.

Celeste walked back to the office. If she put all her focus on the reports, she could be done in two hours. With no interruptions or distractions, she could do it.

It took three tries for her old car to start when she turned the key. One of these days, it wouldn't start for good. Tonight, it made her late even more. By the time she pulled into her parking space next to Filipe's pickup truck, it was almost nine thirty. She exited and noticed a high-back booster seat in his passenger seat. She'd forgotten to get Lucas's seat from her car, which meant Filipe had bought one.

Celeste sent him a text when she got to her apartment door. **I'm here. Could you let me in?**

A few moments later, the sound of steps came closer, then the chain rattled before he opened the door.

He brought a finger to his lips. "It took three bedtime stories, but he's been asleep since eight."

Celeste dropped her purse on the narrow table in the entry and slipped off her shoes. "The little stinker. He took advantage of you."

"He knows I don't mind."

She sat on the sofa and pulled a pillow behind her back, glad for the chance to finally relax.

Filipe sat at the other end. "Was there a problem with one of the animals? Is that why you had to stay longer?" He asked her in a low voice.

"The animals are all fine," Celeste replied in the same tone. "Alice wanted the quarterly evaluations done tonight and turned in tomorrow morning."

Filipe frowned. "She asked you to stay over to do reports that can be done during the day? Why the rush?"

"I honestly don't know."

"Does she ask other employees to stay after hours?"

"No, but it's okay," she replied quickly, hoping he'd move on to something else.

"That seems hardly fair, Celeste. I'll have to ask her about it."

"Please don't. I don't want to antagonize Alice. She is my boss."

If he talked to Alice, it would be even worse. In an effort to distract him, Celeste set a light hand on his forearm. "Tell me, what did you and Lucas do together other than read stories?"

Filipe didn't seem convinced, but he took the change of subject without protesting. He told her about Lucas, the games they'd played before dinner, the food they'd eaten, and all the books they'd looked at.

The more they talked, the more relaxed she became. Somehow, they'd gravitated closer together, hands almost touching but not quite. It was comfortable between them, and everything else about having Filipe in her tiny apartment felt the same.

Was this the right time to bring up the past? He'd done it first when he'd apologized for not being there after Eduardo died but hadn't said anything else about it.

He finished retelling a joke Lucas had told him earlier. "He really is a funny kid."

"I'll have to make it up to you for the time you spent with him," she said.

"You don't have to make up for anything," he said lightly. "I had just as much fun as he did."

Before she lost her nerve, Celeste went for the point-blank approach. "Why did you leave right after Eduardo's funeral?"

His eyes went wide, and he visibly recoiled at her direct question. "Celeste, I—"

"Mamã," came Lucas's voice, "I need help."

Celeste turned to find her son coming down the hallway, rubbing his eyes and pouting.

Filipe stood immediately. "You better go see what he needs. I'll let myself out."

And just like that, he was gone.

"Coming, Lucas," she said, standing from the sofa. "Mommy's coming."

CHAPTER SIX

Celeste stopped and lowered the two buckets she carried to the ground, watching the scene across the yard where Filipe worked with the laborers.

Today was Thursday already and she still didn't know what to tell him about the ride he'd offered. Being in a car with him for two and a half hours might not be the best idea, but her unreliable car had her worried it wouldn't make the trip. Of course, taking the bus was always an option and the intercity to Porto from Peniche had a route running on the weekend.

A shipment of plants had just arrived, and Filipe was helping the nursery workers unload the pallets from the back of the truck.

He wore a dark-blue T-shirt that stretched across his shoulders and chest, and Celeste's imagination filled in the rest of the details. He'd been attractive at nineteen, but at thirty-one he was hot. In the early morning, the sun beat down much too bright already, and Filipe grabbed the hem of his T-shirt to wipe his forehead, exposing a flat stomach and muscled sides.

Hunky piece of halibut. What abs he had. Construction work looked good on him indeed.

When Filipe looked up and caught her staring at him, he smiled and held a hand up in greeting. Celeste kicked one of the buckets at her feet and scrambled to pick it up before it spilled. She straightened in time to see Filipe's knowing smirk. Yes, she'd been checking him out. Too late to pretend she hadn't. She waved back at him, hoping the distance between them was enough to hide the blush on her cheeks.

Just then someone called his name, and Filipe lifted his head in the direction of two men walking his way. They were dressed in business casual clothes and didn't look like they'd come to work. Filipe shook off his hands on the side of his pants and approached them to greet them warmly.

Celeste returned to her work, curious to know who the men were. Despite the shorter hours, she finished her work on time. The party for the employees and their families at the hotel was today, and Filipe let everyone leave an hour earlier to get their family members. She went home to change into a casual dress and sandals and then collected Lucas at daycare. His excitement could hardly be contained, as evidenced by his constant chatter on the way to the SoliMar. Lucas was taken with Filipe, and she couldn't blame him. The way Filipe treated Lucas warmed her heart and had her wishing for things that would never happen.

Celeste parked at the aquarium and walked to the hotel with Lucas's hand in hers. The sounds and chatter of people reached them before they stepped onto the lawn in front of the building. String lights had been hung, already twinkling in the near-waning day, and extra tables and umbrellas brought in to the space around the pool. In a corner, a DJ stood behind a table playing pop music, and parents and children of all ages danced to the upbeat sounds. Celeste greeted her coworkers and introduced Lucas to those who didn't know him.

In the early evening, the sun held out long enough to delay its setting over the waters of the Atlantic. With a light breeze coming in from the beach, the temperature had finally dropped to a comfortable level.

Lucas gave her hand a pull. "Nice party, huh, Mamã?"

"It is a nice party," she replied.

"Where's Filipe? Isn't this his party?"

She'd been wondering where Filipe was, scanning the crowd for his familiar face and not finding him. "He might be busy, Lucas." Lucas wouldn't be the only one disappointed if they left without seeing Filipe. "Are you hungry? Let's get something to eat."

They walked to the manned buffet tables loaded with entrées, sides, and desserts, the latter a popular spot, judging from the way young and old congregated around it. Celeste managed to carry two plates and found a table farther away from the crowd for her and Lucas.

Despite her efforts to distract Lucas with the food, his focus was somewhere else. "Where's Filipe? I really miss him."

A few minutes later, the gait of a man walking in their direction pulled their attention.

"I was wondering where my two favorite people were," Filipe said with a wide smile.

"Filipe!" Lucas ran to him, and Filipe swung him up in the air, both laughing, before setting him down on the grass.

Celeste's heart skipped a beat at the sight in front of her. Filipe wore white slim pants and a tailored navy button shirt, untucked and with the sleeves rolled back. He'd trimmed his beard again, and Celeste's hands itched to touch the side of his face. Instead, she crossed her legs and pulled her hands onto her lap.

Alice stood from a nearby table and walked in front of Celeste, blocking the view. "Look at you, Filipe, playing with your employees' children," she said. "You're such a fun boss."

"Olá, Alice. How are you?" Filipe greeted her in a neutral voice.

"So this is your favorite little guy?" Alice's voice was upbeat and friendly. Celeste froze as Alice stepped closer to Filipe and Lucas.

She had obviously heard Filipe's comment and appeared displeased, perhaps even more than usual.

"This is my buddy Lucas," Filipe replied. "He and I had a great time together the other night, hanging out while Celeste worked late, finishing reports that weren't even due yet."

Alice's fake smile faltered.

"I really appreciate responsible employees who are always where they are supposed to be and are willing to go the extra mile," Filipe continued laying it on, ignoring Celeste's frown and slight shake of her head.

"Well," Alice said awkwardly, glancing back at her table as if wishing she'd never left it. "I'll be going now. Just wanted to say hello." She turned and hurried away before either Celeste or Filipe could respond.

"Goodbye," Lucas called after her.

"Hello nightmare at work tomorrow," Celeste muttered under her breath.

"Pay no attention to her," Filipe said. "I don't." His mischievous grin was irresistible, and Celeste found even Alice woes couldn't dampen the happiness she felt in his presence.

Lucas pulled out a chair, and Filipe sat close enough she could smell his cologne, a mix of sun, salty air, and Filipe's own scent. She was in trouble if he sat this close for the rest of the night.

"Sorry I'm late," he said. "I had a couple of showings that went over today, and it set me back. The important thing is I'm here now and I'm so glad you two came," Filipe said, his eyes on her.

"This is the best party. Even Mamã said so," Lucas said.

Filipe looked at her and she nodded. "I did say that." She was curious to know what he'd meant by showings. "What were you showing?"

"The grounds and buildings of the aquarium. But don't worry. I haven't had any offers yet."

Should she be worried? She'd have to ask him more about it later.

When Lucas put his arm around his shoulders, Filipe pulled him onto his lap and asked about his day. The two talked about it for a few minutes as if they were the best of friends and had known each other for a long time.

Celeste quickly forgot her concerns about the aquarium. A lump of emotion rose in her throat. This was what she wanted for her son—someone who was present and made Lucas feel important. Was that too much to ask? She inhaled, willing her heart to calm down and her mind to dislodge the idea.

Several people approached Filipe to ask questions about the SoliMar or to introduce their family members, and after another interruption, Filipe stood. "How about we go for a walk on the beach before it gets dark?"

Lucas latched on to Filipe's hand, and Celeste took her place on the other side of Lucas.

They weaved through the crowd, stopping several times for Filipe to greet employees and answer brief questions.

Although the beach wasn't empty, if afforded them a sense of privacy they didn't have on the hotel's lawn.

"Is it always like this?" Celeste asked.

Filipe nodded. "Mostly at family-oriented events. I like to make myself available, even if it's a little too much at times. "

Lucas grabbed on to her hand, and the three of them walked together.

"How do you do it?" she asked.

"Do what?"

"Know everyone by name, whatever position they have."

"Something I learned from my Grandpa António. To him, honor and family are paramount. He taught me to respect everyone, whatever kind of work they do. He was the one who impressed on me the importance of shaking someone's hand firmly and looking directly at them. He taught me to always learn the name of the person I'm dealing with. It builds up a relationship."

She'd seen it in the last fifteen minutes. The admiration and respect these people had for Filipe were obvious in their smiles and the way they addressed him. Not only that but they were loyal to him as well.

Since his arrival at the aquarium two weeks ago, Celeste had found herself conflicted. Filipe inspired trust, but he was there only to finish the renovations and sell the aquarium. How could she give him her loyalty with so many changes coming?

"You're taking the bus to Porto?" Filipe asked.

Celeste frowned.

"Lucas just told me you two are taking a trip to see his grandpa and taking the big bus to get there."

She'd been so deep in her thoughts about the man at her side, she'd hardly noticed her son telling Filipe about their plans as he looked for shells along the shore.

"I don't want to put the kilometers on the car," she said. If the car even started.

"Are you sure you don't want to ride with me? I'm already going to Porto that weekend. My cousin Matias is getting married in the morning, and the reception is in the evening. When are you going to see your dad?"

"On Saturday morning."

"That's perfect. You can take my car. I'm in the wedding party all morning and through lunch, and I can catch a ride with my cousins if I need to go anywhere. When you're done, you can join me for the reception."

Celeste shook her head. "I can't come to the wedding." She wasn't part of the family or friends.

"You can come as my guest," Filipe said with a smile. "You'll be doing me a favor." He grimaced. "My mom has been trying to set me up with a blind date for the reception with some daughter of one of her neighbors. If you come, I can tell her I already have someone to go with me."

"Go with you as your date?" She stopped at the suggestion.

Lucas gave her a tug, and she resumed walking, her mind churning with scenarios she hadn't entertained for so long.

"It's just for one evening, and you won't be seeing anyone who'll ask for explanations later. Unless the idea is really that repulsive to you," he added, a surprising hint of vulnerability in his voice.

"No, of course not," she replied. Wasn't dating Filipe what she'd always wanted when they were teenagers?

"I want to go in Filipe's car," Lucas piped up.

She'd thought him distracted with shells on the sand, but of course he'd been paying attention to the conversation.

Filipe arched an eyebrow at her but refrained from commenting.

"Is your car as nice as your truck?" Lucas asked.

"It's much better." Filipe's mouth raised in amusement.

"I'll try not to barf, then," Lucas said in his most serious voice. "One time I felt sick while my mom was driving, but she stopped, and I barfed on the ground outside."

"That's a good idea. You let me know if you feel sick and I'll stop."

Lucas turned to Celeste. "Will the bus stop if I need to barf, Mamã?"

Filipe coughed to hide a chuckle, his smile enough proof of what he thought about Lucas's question.

"No, the bus doesn't stop," she said.

"I think it's better we go in Filipe's car." Lucas smiled, apparently happy with himself for the perfect solution he offered.

"Sounds greats by me," Filipe said.

She looked between them. "You two are ganging up on me."

Lucas laughed as if that was the funniest thing in the world.

And just like that, her five-year-old son had the weekend travels planned for her. In truth, it was convenient to have Lucas as an excuse to give in to what she really wanted to do anyway.

Of course, that also meant she'd be pretending to be Filipe's date to his cousin's wedding.

As if going to see her father weren't stressful enough.

They left from Peniche early in the morning just as rosy hues streaked across the gray sky. Filipe drove steadily, and Lucas fell asleep after thirty minutes of driving, much to Celeste's relief.

For a man of his means, Filipe didn't like to show off. She'd seen him drive a pickup truck when he came to the aquarium, but he'd come to get her and Lucas at the apartment in a sleek black sedan. It was a newer model but not the latest, and comfort, style, and safety, instead of status, seemed more important to him. Lucas had been impressed with the built-in child seat, and so had she.

She took a fortifying breath. Taking advantage of a sleeping Lucas in the back seat, this was the perfect time to talk to Filipe.

Celeste cleared her throat. "I talked to Lucas about my father, but I didn't go into much detail."

"They've never met, right?" Filipe asked.

She shook her head. "No. I think I'm going to need to tell Lucas a little more of what this visit means." She sighed. "I feel like I haven't prepared him well enough."

"I'll leave you two alone when we get to the hotel."

Celeste turned to him. "You don't have to do that. Lucas is comfortable with you." Even if Filipe's presence didn't help, it certainly wouldn't hinder. "I just don't want to add to his confusion." Introducing a man who was related to him but not present on a daily basis—how would that affect Lucas? Was he old enough to understand?

What about the man sitting next to her? There was another talk she needed to have.

"What about you and me, Filipe?" she asked without preamble.

A slight wince pulled at his expression, but he quickly hid it. "What about you and me?"

Celeste tilted her head and looked at him without saying a word. He knew very well what she meant.

Filipe quickly glanced at the back seat and then let out a long sigh. "I guess you want to have that talk now since Lucas is sleeping."

It would be a good time for it. Was she ready to put everything on the line? Expose her heart to Filipe and hope he didn't trample it again? Was there ever a good time for such a vulnerable, difficult talk? "Ever since we met again, I've been trying to understand what happened back then, but I can't do that until I know your side."

He nodded. "I've been trying to do the same, but I guess saying I was young and dumb isn't enough, is it?"

"It's a start," she said.

His expression lightened for a moment. "I never meant to hurt you, Celeste." He glanced at her.

"We were all hurting after Eduardo passed away," she agreed.

"I knew that. Believe me, I knew that really well. Burdening you with more pain was never what I wanted."

As much as she wanted to prompt him to keep talking, she gave him space and waited for him to continue.

The shrill of Filipe's phone ringing interrupted them. He glanced at her with an apologetic expression. "Answer phone," he said, and the call connected. "Hello, this is Filipe Romano."

"Senhor Romano," a man's voice said. "This is Victor Abrantes. Any chance we could meet today before I leave the area? I'd like to discuss the acquisition of the SoliMar Aquarium."

Celeste's eyes snapped up to Filipe, and he winced.

"I'm sorry, Senhor Abrantes. I'm out of town for the weekend," he said to the man. "I'll have my manager give you a call on Monday."

The man agreed and they hung up.

The question flew out of her mouth. "You're selling the aquarium?"

Filipe let out a long sigh. "I don't know what I'm doing yet, Celeste. From a business perspective, it makes no sense to keep it. But when I see Lucas with the birds..."

Celeste looked back at Lucas, who still slept. "I thought you'd changed your mind about selling," she said in a low voice, trying to keep the emotion out of it. "Those men that came to see you earlier in the week were buyers, weren't they?"

"There were just looking," he said warily. "I haven't made any decisions."

She only nodded, unable to summon any appropriate words. What was she going to do if Filipe went ahead with the sale and the new owners converted the aquarium to something else? Where would she work?

The answers threatened a headache. This was so not what she wanted for today. She relaxed her tension-filled shoulders and looked out the passenger's side window at the passing landscape, purposely emptying her mind of the worries and problems that seemed to plague her lately.

After a few minutes, Filipe switched the radio to a soft music station on low volume, and Celeste relaxed in the comfortable seat. There was nothing else she could do for now. At one point, she rested her eyes for a moment, only to wake when they arrived at the hotel where the Romanos were staying.

He pulled into the front, and two valets came to open the doors. "Welcome to the River View, Senhor Romano."

"Thanks, Roberto." Filipe handed him the key to his car. "Please have the luggage delivered and the car parked in the short-term space. The lady will be taking it out after breakfast."

While Celeste exited, Filipe came around, unbuckled a sleepy Lucas, and carried him in. She followed, still trying to adjust. Filipe knew the valet's name. Did that mean he came here often?

Unbeknownst to her, Filipe had booked a room for her and Lucas, right across from his suite on the top floor.

When she raised an eyebrow at him, he simply shrugged. "This way you can freshen up and have breakfast before you go see your father." Filipe set Lucas down on the plush sofa in the large room. "I was also thinking of me, so we can have a good night's rest and leave Sunday morning."

At least Celeste was prepared to spend the night, even if it hadn't occurred to her. She'd brought a small bag for her and Lucas with more formal clothes they could change into for the wedding later. Going to see her dad in a dress was definitely not a good idea.

The place dripped with elegance and luxury. Most likely, she couldn't afford one night here, let alone two.

"And before you go thinking about how much it costs, it's part of a conglomerate I'm in."

He must have seen the question on her expression. "What does that mean?" she asked.

"It's like a network of hotel owners. I'm not paying full rates."

Probably because he owned part of it.

Lucas was now fully awake and trying to climb on the bed.

Filipe sat next to him. "I hope you're hungry, Lucas, 'cause I'm starved." He patted his stomach in a dramatic gesture.

Lucas rubbed his belly. "I'm starffed too," he said.

Celeste smiled. They'd become such good friends.

After breakfast, Filipe let Celeste drive the car around the parking lot to become familiar with it.

"I should have brought my car," she said, unable to hide her nerves. "This one is too nice for me to drive."

Filipe set a hand on top of hers. "Relax. It's fully insured. I feel much better knowing you two will be better protected."

"Thank you," she said again. She'd thanked him a few times already, but it didn't seem enough.

"Call me if you need anything," Filipe said before exiting. "Otherwise, I'll see you two later today." He leaned in a fraction, as if to brush a kiss on her cheek, but paused halfway and squeezed her shoulder instead. Then he turned to Lucas and high-fived him.

As Celeste drove away, she watched Filipe through the rearview mirror, standing on the sidewalk with his hands in his pockets.

"Why didn't Filipe come with us?" Lucas asked.

"He's going to his cousin's wedding, and we're going to see your grandfather, Avô Pedro." She met Lucas's eyes in the rear view mirror. "Remember how I told you about him?"

He nodded. "He's your father."

"That's right, he is. But I haven't seen him in a while."

"Because he made some bad choices," Lucas said.

He remembered more than she'd thought he might. "He's my father and I love him, but I don't agree with some of the things he's done in the past."

"If he says something you don't like, we're going to leave right away," Lucas said.

It always impressed her how good a memory he had. "You're such a smart boy, Lucas." She smiled at him, and he smiled back.

He was soon distracted by the view outside the window.

The Saturday morning traffic was light, much to Celeste's relief, and the drive took less time than she'd expected.

Celeste approached the clinic and followed the signs to the parking on the left side of the building. Three stories high, simple architecture, and overall discreet. No signage announcing what they did inside, which was obviously on purpose.

Once inside, the age and wear of the building were harder to disguise, and although clean, it could have used some updates. She waited until a staff member came, then introduced herself and was told where to find her father in the backyard.

Celeste gripped Lucas's hand, a flash of doubt coursing through her. Maybe she should have come alone instead of subjecting her son to a possibly stressful situation. She'd considered leaving him with Hugo, but Hugo hadn't returned her call, as usual. What if something didn't go well? She hadn't seen her father in over three years, since just before Lucas's second birthday. What would he look like?

She walked past the back porch and down the few steps. A group of tables and outdoor chairs sat under the shade of two large trees, and a few people visited casually.

"Where's your dad?" Lucas asked.

"I'm not sure." She looked around again just as a man stood and walked in their direction.

At first she didn't recognize him. He looked like he'd aged ten years and not the mere three since she'd last seen him. All his hair had turned white, and his bearing was not as straight as it had once been. His eyes looked clear, though, and that was a difference she welcomed.

"Celeste." His voice was uncertain. "I wasn't sure you'd come."

She took a step forward and brushed a kiss against his cheek, at which his posture relaxed. "It's good to see you, Dad."

Celeste stepped back and placed her hands on Lucas's shoulders. "You remember Lucas?"

"I remember him but not like this. He's so grown up."

Lucas tilted his head. "Are you my grandpa?"

"This is your Avô Pedro I told you about," she said.

Her dad smiled but his eyes were luminous with unshed tears. "Do you like to play ball?"

They followed him to a table at the far corner, where he handed a small red ball to Lucas. After tossing it back and forth with Lucas for a few minutes, he joined Celeste at the table while Lucas played by himself on the grass.

Celeste breathed out in relief. So far, so good. Her father was behaving normally, and so was her son. Maybe she could put her fears aside for now.

He took the seat across from her. "Your little guy has grown into a handsome child. Smart too." He paused. "You look well. How is life treating you? And that husband of yours, he didn't come?"

"I've been divorced for a while, Dad. Do you remember?"

He shrugged. "You're better off then. I never did like that guy too much."

Now he told her. He'd been quiet when she and Hugo had announced they were expecting and getting married. Even if her dad had said anything against it, she wouldn't have changed her mind back then, blinded by optimism and impending motherhood.

Celeste glanced in Lucas's direction, but he hadn't heard her father's comment. "How are you?"

"Better than the last time you saw me, I bet," he said in a self-deprecating tone.

The humor in his eyes was hard to resist, and she nodded.

"What are you doing now?"

"Still at the aquarium. I like it there." Hopefully she could convince Filipe to open it again instead of selling.

"What about friends? Do you go out and have fun?"

"I'm a single mother. I don't have time for that."

Her father frowned. "You're still young. Having fun is good for you." He cocked his head and watched her for a moment. "No friends at all?"

"Do you remember Eduardo's friend? Filipe Romano?"

He nodded slowly. "Those two were thick as thieves."

"He owns the aquarium where I work. And the rest of the resort too."

"Really? I guess he did well for himself."

She cleared her throat. "We actually drove up with him. One of his cousins is getting married today."

"What about him? Is he married?"

"No." She didn't want to wonder why Filipe had never married.

"Good. Maybe you two might still have a chance, if you can forgive him for breaking your heart."

Heat rose in her neck. "It wasn't like that." She was lying, of course. It had been like that.

"Your mom always said you two would end up together someday."

Celeste froze, a knot of emotion bubbling up in her chest. "She did?"

"Several times."

She blinked and looked away, unwilling to think of her mom and what she'd thought of Filipe. Could it be true? Did she and Filipe have any chance? "Enough about me. How are you really doing?"

"Trying to get my life in order." He looked up and tipped his chin toward the building. "This place is good for that."

"How much longer will you be here?"

"As long as I need to." He paused and fidgeted with a fleck of paint on the table. "I asked you to come so I could apologize to you." Celeste shook her head, but he raised a hand, asking her to keep quiet. "When your mother died, I lost it. She'd been keeping everything going after Eduardo's accident, and I couldn't cope with not having her around, not having both of them."

Celeste wiped a tear at the corner of her eye. She'd felt the same way, with her brother gone and Filipe too—then her mother a year later.

"I'm sorry I wasn't there for you," her father said.

Celeste reached a hand and covered his fingers with hers. "I'm glad you asked us to come."

CHAPTER SEVEN

Filipe had been waiting all day for Celeste and Lucas to arrive. That was part of his problem, since they wouldn't be getting to the reception until later. She'd sent him a text saying they'd be a little longer than she'd thought as they were having lunch with her father and taking Lucas for a tram ride around the city of Porto.

Filipe sat at the table closest to the entrance, his chair sideways so he could keep an eye on the party and not miss anyone newly arrived. His jacket draped the back of his chair, and he'd loosened his tie and rolled up his sleeves to his elbows. Every few minutes he checked his phone for incoming messages, but nothing showed on the screen.

He almost wished he'd gone with them, but of course he wouldn't miss Matias's wedding and the Romano get-together. He wasn't worried Celeste wouldn't come; he only wanted her to come sooner so they could spend more time together.

The reception had started two hours before for family and close friends with a sit-down dinner. Everyone else would start trailing in soon for the buffet dinner, with the dancing expected to last until much later. Of course, the bride and groom would leave before then. Matias had told Filipe he had a surprise for his bride and they'd be leaving on a private boat for their honeymoon. The perks of being a river boat captain.

In the morning, the wedding had gone smoothly, as far as he could tell. Matias and Vanessa only had eyes for each other, despite the throngs of onlookers and journalists waiting outside the church. As the granddaughter and heiress to the cruise ship magnate António Valadares, Vanessa attracted the attention of the media, and the wedding had been dubbed the most anticipated of the year at the national level. It seemed no expense had been spared. Of course, the media loved to photograph Matias and Vanessa on any occasion—the way they cut such contrasting, attractive figures, him with dark hair and her with blonde—and even more so on their wedding day.

At least the event had brought the Romanos together, along with hordes of other cousins. There was nothing the lot of them liked more than a family reunion—the more the better—especially under the excuse of a wedding with lots of food, drink, and dancing into the night.

Matias appeared calm enough, aside from the slight twitch of his jaw every once in a while. He'd confided in Filipe that he would have preferred a smaller, more intimate ceremony, but with Vanessa's grandparents planning and hosting the wedding, that was a hollow wish on Matias's part. Vanessa looked radiant, unfazed by all the attention, with genuine happiness in her expression. If Filipe didn't like Matias and Vanessa so much, he would have had a hard time being patient, if not a little jealous of them for finding each other.

Not to mention his other cousins who'd tied the knot recently. Catarina had been the first one, on the first day of the year. She and her husband Afonso and their baby girl Carlota were happy as well. Jacinta and Knox had married less than two months ago, and they had the same lovesick look on their faces as the bride and groom. It must be something contagious.

If only Filipe could catch the same.

He'd thrown it all away when he was young and stupid. Now he'd found Celeste again, but it was too late for them. Wasn't it?

His mom approached and took the chair next to him. "Still waiting on that girl of yours?"

She wasn't really his girl. He only wished she were. "She'll be here soon."

"Have we met her before?" his mom asked.

"Do you remember Eduardo Quintano?"

"Your friend from high school? That poor boy. Such a tragedy." She made the sign of the cross. "And his poor family too."

Filipe winced at his mother's gesture, as appropriate as it was. "It's his sister, Celeste. The girl who came with me."

His mom's eyes went wide. "Celeste Quintano is your date to the wedding? How did that happen?"

"She works at the aquarium that was included with the purchase of the hotel in Peniche, and her surname is Ferreira now."

"Such a small world," his mom said, a sense of awe in her words. "Why did she change her name?"

"Celeste is divorced and has a five-year-old son."

"How good are things between you? Any long-term plans?" Just like his mom, to try and find everything she could in one sitting.

"It's complicated." Filipe rubbed the back of his neck. "Please don't make any comments when she gets here. It's not the right place or time for that kind of suggestion."

His mother raised her palms in a placating gesture. "I won't suggest anything. But I'd like to greet her." From a nearby table, his aunt Glória gestured at his mother, and she rose.

"Mãe," he called, and she stopped. "One more thing. Don't ask about her parents. Her mother passed away a year after her brother and her father has health issues."

She brought a hand over her chest. "The poor girl," she said, then left to see her sister-in-law.

If Filipe hadn't said anything to his mother about Celeste's family, she would have surely asked Celeste about them. It was easier to avoid a few awkward minutes this way.

His phone vibrated in his pocket, and Filipe hurried to retrieve it.

We're here. Can you come meet us at the entrance?

Celeste. His heart tripped.

Be right there.

He grabbed the suit jacket from the back of the chair, straightened his sleeves, and quickly slipped the jacket on as he made his way to the front of the hotel.

Celeste and Lucas stood in the lobby, and at the sight of them, Filipe's expression widened in a grin.

Celeste wore a pink floral dress with short sleeves and a flowy hem that grazed her knees and showed off her shapely legs. Her hair was down in simple waves, almost brushing her shoulders, as she used to wear it when she was younger. Only this was a woman beside him, and he liked the way she'd aged into soft curves and gentle planes. Motherhood had changed her appearance, and it looked good on her. The way she'd felt in his arms last week was not enough—he wanted more. Would she dance with him if he asked?

"Your favorite people are here, Filipe," Lucas said.

His mother chuckled, and Filipe joined her. "I'm so glad you are." Something in Celeste's eyes made him pause. "How did it go with your dad?"

She met his eyes. "It was good. I'll tell you more later."

He'd have to wait until she was ready to talk. For now, he steered them in. "Come on, let me introduce you to my cousin and his new wife."

Celeste leaned toward Filipe. "You didn't tell me your cousin's new wife is the heiress to the Gold River Cruises," she whispered in his ear. "Good thing I googled it. This was the best I could do on short notice." She gestured to Lucas and herself.

Her breath touched the side of his ear and his skin broke into goose bumps. Filipe placed a gentle hand at the small of her back and urged her forward, trying to put some distance between them. As much as he wanted to get closer to her, their relationship was not there yet. "You and Lucas look great. Don't worry about it."

"I didn't bring a gift either," she added.

Filipe glanced at her. "I took care of that."

She arched an eyebrow in reply but quickly got distracted when they entered the reception room.

Lucas's attention shifted immediately to the dessert table, which offered American candy and sweets and an ice cream bar with all the toppings, along with the traditional Portuguese wedding desserts.

As Lucas tried to make a run for it, Celeste grabbed his arm. "Not so fast, little guy." She crouched to his level and tipped her chin toward the newlyweds. "We're going to meet Filipe's cousin first. Then you'll get some dinner, and if you eat all your vegetables, we'll talk about dessert."

Lucas's shoulders slumped for a moment, but he

soon perked up when he saw some of his favorite food laid out on the buffet.

After meeting Matias and Vanessa and waiting for Celeste and Lucas to fill their plates, Filipe took them to a table, and they sat down to eat.

"Big wedding," she said as she looked around.

Filipe agreed. "Lots of family on both sides. Speaking of which." Filipe's mom and Tia Glória approached, and Filipe stood to make introductions.

He should have known they'd be too curious not to come over.

If only he and Celeste weren't pretending to be together.

Celeste could hardly keep up with the names of Filipe's cousins and other family members who came to introduce themselves. Matias and Vanessa were the newlyweds; she remembered that well. In spite of having Portuguese family, the bride had been raised in the United States and was still learning Portuguese.

One of Filipe's girl cousins had married an American who'd moved to Porto, and Filipe's sister Luciana was there with her American boyfriend. The American and Portuguese international relations were in good standing with this family. Another of the girl cousins had married the classic pianist Afonso Cortez, and they had a darling baby girl whom Celeste wished to hold but didn't have the courage to ask.

There were too many of the single cousins to remember their names. Filipe also introduced her to his grandparents, and his parents remembered her well. From the look on their faces and lack of questions about her family, Filipe had most likely told them about her mom and dad. Probably better that way. It wasn't the best place to talk about depressing subjects.

Despite some brief, uncomfortable moments, when people assumed she and Filipe were a couple, Celeste was glad she'd come. They stuck to their story that she was Filipe's date, and nobody questioned it, taking it as completely normal.

Lucas thrived with the attention. Other than the baby girl, Filipe's siblings and cousins didn't have young children, but there were plenty from other branches of the family and Vanessa's as well, which included boys and girls close to Lucas's age. Filipe took him around to meet the other children and stayed with him until Lucas felt more at ease. The way Lucas laughed and played with them lifted her worry for him.

While she looked around the room, observing the people and the way they interacted, the atmosphere was loud and even somewhat disorganized. But the love and care they had for one another trumped anything else, resulting in a light, happy mood.

This was the kind of family she'd always wanted. As obnoxious and intruding as large families could be, the support they gave one another made up for the inconveniences. In truth, only people with large families complained about large families. The rest of the world admired and envied them from afar, just as she did right now, and from the way she kept to herself and didn't socialize much, no one would guess that of her.

Eduardo's accident had changed everything.

The emotion hit her, knotting her chest tightly. Celeste rose from her chair and forced the maudlin thoughts away, postponing them for a private moment of self-pity.

She went to the bar and asked for a cold bottle of passion fruit soda, keeping her eyes on Lucas and Filipe. Just then, Filipe turned and locked his gaze on her, the corner of his mouth raising in a smile. He winked, then talked to the young women in the group and introduced Lucas to them.

As she wondered what Filipe was up to, he crossed the room to her.

Celeste's pulse quickened at the way he watched her, and her cheeks flamed at the intent she saw in his eyes. And that dark-blue suit he wore—it should be a crime for a man to look that good. He should have definitely worn it more often.

The tailored cut emphasized his wide shoulders and trim waist, and the rich tone of the fabric enhanced the color of his eyes. All the Romano men wore matching suits and they looked like Italian models at fashion week.

Filipe leaned close to her and tipped his chin toward Lucas and the young woman. "Those are my cousins Anita and Susana. They're taking the little kids to one of the suites to watch movies. They love little kids. Lucas is in good hands."

"I trust you," she said.

"Come dance with me."

"I haven't danced in so long," Celeste said.

"It'll come back to you." He took her hand and led her to the dance floor, where they joined other couples already there.

The live band wrapped up a popular song with a fast beat and quickly segued into a slow dance. When Filipe rested a hand on her waist, Celeste shivered. She lifted a hand to his shoulder, and Filipe brought her closer to him. Through it all, Filipe kept eye contact with her until they settled in each other's arms and started dancing.

She'd never danced with Filipe before he left all those years ago, and not for lack of wishing. That last summer they spent together, their relationship had been escalating from the adolescent friendship they'd had for years to something more that neither of them was ready to acknowledge. Not until the night when everything had changed.

How many times had she danced with Hugo? Maybe a couple of times before her pregnancy with Lucas, then once at their wedding. None with the emotional charge she felt right now.

"Finally," Filipe murmured in her ear. "I've been wanting to dance with you since you were fifteen."

She pulled away to glance at him. "That long, huh?

"Why the skepticism? I had a crush on you since the day we met."

She swallowed. "You never said anything."

The corner of his lips quirked. "Of course not. I was a teenage boy infatuated with my best friend's little sister. I couldn't let anyone know, least of all you."

She'd felt the same way for a long time and hadn't confided in anyone either. So much time wasted.

Filipe nuzzled the side of her neck, and a deep warmth spread from her chest. His scent enveloped her, tightening the pull toward him, a deep wave of attraction rising within her. The music became an afterthought as her mind and heart focused on the man holding her.

Why did it feel so right?

What about her mom's prediction about her and Filipe ending up together?

Gradually, Filipe guided them past the double doors, and they danced away to a more secluded corner. Even after the music changed back to something with a faster beat, they remained in each other's arms, swaying gently to a silent song.

The night was warm, and a half-moon hung in the dark-blue sky. The hotel stood on a hill at the edge of the city and the view extended to the Douro River below. From a nearby garden, the heady scent of wisteria carried in on the gentle breeze. It was the perfect kind of night for a wedding reception, one that would stay in the memories of the bride and groom.

When Filipe brushed his lips along her jaw, Celeste held her breath. Something warred inside her for a moment, a feeling between wanting to be closer to Filipe and needing to preserve her heart intact. But as he kissed her in the spot behind her ear, she tipped her neck to give him better access and pushed her worries away.

Filipe pulled back a fraction and hesitated to give her time to push away, to ask her for permission—whatever it was, she didn't want the distance. Celeste grabbed his lapels until his lips met her mouth.

Finally.

This was what she needed, what she'd always wanted.

A blast of sensations rushed through her—the pressure of his lips on hers, his hands holding her hips, the scent of his cologne all around her, on her.

"It's been so long," he whispered against her mouth.

Celeste tightened her arms around his neck, holding on to him on unsteady legs.

It was new, and it was coming home, all rolled into one.

She couldn't say how long it lasted, a string of shorter kisses leading up to a longer one. When the heat between them intensified, Filipe slowly spaced his kisses until they stopped, then rested his forehead against hers.

"I should have never left you," Filipe said.

But he had. He'd left her without a word, without ever looking for her or making any contact in all the years that followed.

Celeste dropped her hands to his and pulled them away from her waist. "Why did you leave?"

She had to know. What would she do if she fell for him again and he left like he had before? And this time, there was more than only her feelings to consider. Lucas was involved as well, and she wouldn't tolerate another man who was quick to put him aside.

As she took a breath and glanced away, Filipe tried to catch her eye. "I'm sorry. Maybe it's too early for a kiss, but I—"

"Not just the kiss," she interrupted. "This thing. Between us. I'm not ready to pick up where we left off twelve years ago without an explanation." Celeste took a step away from him, already feeling the loss of his body against hers. "Maybe coming was a mistake."

"Why would you say that?"

"You pushed me to come to the reception, to do this weekend with you when I wasn't ready."

"I wanted you to come, yes. I thought I could help you by offering you a ride with me, thought it could be more fun. But I didn't push you to do anything you didn't want to yourself. We're consenting adults, Celeste. And I'm pretty sure we both want the same thing."

He was right, of course. Somehow, she didn't feel any better about it.

"Maybe I don't know everything I want, but I know I don't want you to hurt me again. I don't want to wake up one day and find you gone."

"I didn't plan it that way." His voice lowered an octave. "I was scared and feeling guilty—"

"You left me at the time I needed you the most. First, my brother was gone, and then my best friend. How did you think that made me feel?" She paused to take a breath, the meaning of his words finally registering. "Wait. Guilty? Why did you feel guilty?"

Filipe turned around and hung his head, then rubbed the side of his forehead.

Celeste stepped in front of him. "Guilt for what, Filipe?"

He let out a long breath. "I guess it's about time I tell you." He started pacing, hands in his pockets. "That night. I asked you out, and I had it all planed." He scoffed. "Nothing was getting in the way of me kissing you."

Celeste stood to the side and nodded, encouraging him to go on. She remembered how excited she'd been when Filipe had asked her out. He'd been very insistent it was a date, but he didn't want Eduardo to know. Up until then, the three of them had always done everything together, and, despite her reservations, she'd agreed to go with Filipe.

He had been nineteen and she'd just turned seventeen, and had been dreaming of going out with him since she was fourteen. Deep down, she knew he was planning to kiss her, and she wanted the same. She would have agreed to almost anything he'd asked.

"I'd been lying to your brother all summer, you know? He knew I had feelings for you, but I denied it every time he asked."

"He never said anything to me," she said.

"He wouldn't have. It would have changed everything between the three of us. That night, Eduardo called a few minutes before I was leaving to pick you up. He wanted to go somewhere with me and take the car, but I told him no."

Filipe had shown up on time, and if he'd been nervous, she hadn't noticed. Somehow, she'd guessed he'd planned to kiss her, and that was all she could think about.

"Of course you didn't go with him," she said. "We met, and you drove me to the hill in your grandparents' village. And you kissed me there."

Filipe passed a careless hand through his hair. "Don't you see, Celeste? He took the motorcycle because I had the car. If I'd gone with him..."

If Filipe had gone with Eduardo, would that have prevented Eduardo's death? Or would both of them have died? A drunk driver had run a red light and crashed into Eduardo. It had been that quick. If Filipe and Eduardo had been crossing that intersection, they both would have been hit.

Filipe closed his eyes and drew in a ragged breath. "He died because I didn't go with him, Celeste. I let my best friend get on that motorcycle, and I was glad he did because I wanted to be alone with you."

Did he even know about the investigation? The police had taken a month, and by then Filipe had been long gone.

"Filipe, there was more than just letting Eduardo on the motorcycle. The drunk driver never even tried to brake."

He frowned. "What drunk driver?"

This time it was Celeste who led him by the hand to the closest bench. They sat down, knees touching, hands still clasped.

"The police investigation of the accident concluded that a drunk driver ran the stop sign, and he didn't even try to slow down or brake, let alone stop."

"So it wasn't Eduardo being reckless?" Filipe asked.

"No, he didn't drive recklessly that night," she replied. "A drunk driver hit him and fled the scene. It took the police two weeks to find him and another two for the final report to come in. But by then you were gone already."

Filipe turned to her, the shock of the news filling his eyes with myriad feelings as he clearly struggled to process the information.

"I never knew—"

"Excuse me?" A voice interrupted them.

Celeste and Filipe turned and found one of his girl cousins holding a teary-eyed Lucas by the hand.

"Is everything all right, sweetie?" Celeste walked over and knelt by her son.

Lucas rubbed at his face. "I got scared when I woke up and didn't see you."

He must have fallen asleep and woken up disoriented.

She pulled him close for a hug. "I'm here."

Celeste rose and took Lucas's hand. When she looked back at Filipe, he motioned for her to go, and she nodded.

They'd have to finish their conversation later.

Lucas fell asleep almost immediately after she put him in bed in their hotel droom.

If only sleep could come that quick for her.

After changing into her pajamas, Celeste sat on the sofa and pulled her knees up, trying to comfort herself as memories of the evening flashed in her mind. Everything had been near perfect—Filipe's family was perfect, flaws and all, and they treated her and Lucas so kindly.

This is what she'd always wanted for her son— doting grandparents, aunts and uncles who spoiled him, an enormity of cousins to play and grow up with. And even brothers and sisters to love.

The Romanos were the example of what it was like to have two parents living together and loving each other and their children—exactly what Celeste wanted for Lucas. For her.

It was fate teasing her, to have it all so close and so out of her reach.

CHAPTER EIGHT

$\mathcal{F}$ilipe had been calling Celeste's phone since Sunday morning without a reply.

On Saturday night, after Anita showed up with Lucas, Celeste had left with her son and hadn't returned. Of course Lucas was more important, and he had needed the comfort of his mother in a strange environment. Filipe couldn't fault either one of them for the interruption.

He hardly slept all night, wrung out with emotions in the wake of the revelations from the night before. As soon as he read 7:00 A.M. on his phone display, he sent her a message. Celeste didn't reply. She didn't reply to the next message or the phone call either. Was everything okay? Should he give them space or check on them?

When he knocked at the door across from his, it was only to discover she'd checked out early in the morning and had left in a taxi.

He was too late. For now, anyway.

He showered, dressed, met his family in the breakfast room, and spent some time with the rest of his extended family that hadn't gone home yet. It would probably be a while before the Romanos got together, and he didn't want to miss seeing anyone.

All the while he was thinking about the way Celeste had kissed him back. That, and how she didn't blame him for her brother's death. If that kiss was any indication, she had feelings for him too.

She finally answered the phone as he pulled into Peniche on Sunday evening.

"Hello?" Her voice sounded feeble and distant.

"I've been trying to reach you all day. Is everything okay with you and Lucas?"

"We're sick. Can I talk to you tomorrow?"

"You're both sick? What happened?" Worry rose inside him. "Can I come over to help?"

"Not now. I gotta go. Lucas is throwing up again."

The line went dead. Filipe glanced at the screen on the console, making sure it wasn't a connection issue.

Instead of retiring to his suite when he got to the hotel, he called ahead to the chef and asked for a container of soup, then found himself at Celeste's building, ringing the bell to her apartment.

The intercom crackled. "Who is it?" Celeste asked, her voice not quite at its normal.

"It's Filipe. Can you ring me up?"

Her lack of response almost had him ringing the bell a second time, but just then the release button sounded, and the door to the building opened. Filipe climbed the stairs to the second floor, balancing the bags in his hands and being careful not to spill. When he arrived at her door, he knocked softly.

The sound of shuffling steps gradually approached until the door opened a crack. Celeste peeked out, then closed the door again, and he heard the jangling of the chain being lifted. When Filipe entered, Celeste was already walking back down a hallway where Lucas cried quietly. Filipe closed the door behind him.

"What are you doing here, Filipe? I called Hugo hours ago. I thought it was him," she said over her shoulder. "I'm too tired to talk with you, and I have to clean the mess Lucas made in his bedroom."

A tabletop lamp illuminated the living room, and Filipe looked around, trying to adjust his eyes to the low ambient light. He placed the containers of soup and the bottles on the counter in the kitchen, then went looking for Celeste, whom he found kneeling on the floor, peeling off Lucas's socks.

The boy looked miserable, with fat tears rolling down his cheeks and a mess down the front of his pajamas. He momentarily stopped crying when Filipe entered, visibly surprised to see him there. From the way her body bent as she struggled to undress her son, Celeste didn't seem to be in much better condition than Lucas.

At the sight of both of them so sick, Filipe's heart squeezed in his chest with empathy and affection.

Maybe when she was feeling better Celeste would chide him for coming, but for now Filipe could only feel relief for being there to offer his help.

He stepped forward and addressed Lucas. "Hey, buddy. I'm so sorry you're not feeling well. Do you mind if I help you get cleaned up while your mom goes to rest?"

Lucas wiped his pale face with a quick hand and shook his head.

Celeste sighed and eyed Filipe warily, leaning against the edge of the mattress.

Filipe helped her to her feet. "I brought rice broth and a bottle of electrolyte replacement. The soup is still warm. Go eat some, and then get in bed. I'll take care of Lucas."

She opened her mouth as if to say something, but then closed it and only nodded in reply.

Filipe set to work with Lucas, talking in low tones. He took the boy to the bathroom and ran the water to a warm bath, then helped Lucas out of his soiled clothes. After helping him wash, he wrapped him in a large towel and sat him on the chair in his bedroom while Filipe stripped the dirty sheets. He balled them up and dropped them on the floor.

"Lucas, where I can find clean pajamas for you?"

Lucas jutted his chin. "In the bottom drawer."

Filipe helped him dry off and get dressed into the clean pajamas, then asked him where to find the sheets. After making the bed, he helped the boy into it.

"Is your tummy feeling better?"

"A little." Lucas settled on his pillow.

Filipe knelt by the bed. "Would you like something to eat?"

Lucas shook his head. "I'm not hungry."

"I'll get you something to drink. I'll be right back."

When he returned, he helped Lucas take a few sips and then tucked him in.

"Will you stay with me until I fall asleep?" Lucas asked as he struggled to keep his eyes open.

"Of course." Filipe sat on the bed, and a little hand sneaked from under the sheets to grab Filipe's fingers.

A swell of emotion rose to Filipe's throat as he held Lucas's warm hand. He trusted so easily and completely. Filipe wanted to protect him and keep him safe.

Within a couple of minutes, Lucas slept soundly. Filipe waited a moment longer, then slipped his hand from Lucas's fingers and rose from the bed. He located Celeste's cleaning supplies and cleaned the floor in Lucas's bedroom. The boy slept peacefully, and a healthy color had returned to his cheeks. Filipe cracked the window open to let in a breeze, pushed the door to his bedroom ajar, and returned the supplies to the kitchen.

On the counter, one of the bottles had been emptied, but the soup remained untouched. He found Celeste sleeping on a stuffed chair in the living room, her neck at an uncomfortable angle. As much as he hated to wake her up, she would be much better in her bed.

"Come on, Celeste, let's put you to bed." It was nearly midnight, and she needed to rest.

She opened her eyes and frowned slightly. "Lucas?"

"He's fine. He's sleeping."

Her shoulders relaxed, and she didn't resist him as helped her to her bedroom and under the sheets. As he tucked her in, Celeste gave his hand a squeeze. "Thank you for taking care of us when you didn't have to," she said in a raspy voice.

Filipe tucked her hair behind her ear with his free hand. "I didn't have to, but I wanted to. And you're welcome. I only wish you'd let me do more." Then he bent and kissed her forehead. She didn't reply to his comment, and he wondered if she'd heard his words at all. When he pulled away, the half smile on Celeste's mouth tugged at his heart.

He already knew he'd fallen for Celeste again, but tonight had only confirmed it. This is what he wanted—to love her, to love them both, to take care of them and be a part of their lives. Celeste didn't trust easily like Lucas did, and Filipe couldn't blame her. Somehow, he had to find a way to make amends for his past actions and earn his right to belong with them. It felt true, and he was determined to make it right this time.

On the way back from getting Lucas's sheets to toss in the washer, the doorbell rang and Filipe paused. Was Celeste expecting anyone?

When he peered through the peephole, a man stood on the other side. Filipe squared his shoulders and opened the door.

"Who are you?" the guy asked immediately.

"I'm Filipe. Who are you?"

"I'm Hugo. What are you doing here?" His tone was decidedly impolite as he looked Filipe up and down as if measuring some sort of competition.

"You're Lucas's father?" Filipe looked over the other man, much shorter than himself.

His clothes were rumpled and had several stains, and his overall appearance was that of a man who didn't care too much for the way he looked. He smelled of stale tobacco, and his long hair was greasy. And this was the man who Lucas called father?

"Yeah. Or at least that's what she told me," Hugo snickered.

It took all of Filipe's self-control to not punch him. "I've known Celeste a long time. She's not that kind of woman." Though how she'd become involved with the likes of this guy was beyond him.

The jealousy nearly blinded Filipe. If it weren't for the mistakes he'd made in the past, for leaving after Eduardo's death, for all the years he'd been away from Celeste without making any effort to contact her—he could have married her first. Instead, she'd married this guy, who obviously didn't appreciate her or their son, and who only caused her worries.

The thought made Filipe mad, mostly at himself.

"I'm here to pick up our kid. Celeste said he's sick."

"He is." Struck with sudden inspiration, Filipe thrust the barf-filled sheets at Hugo. "He's been throwing up. When you're finished washing these, his rug needs to be cleaned too."

A look of revulsion crossed Hugo's face. He tossed the sheets back at Filipe, taking a step back. "I'm not the maid."

"No. Just a dad, and a lousy one at that," Filipe said, not caring to hold back his opinion. "Celeste called you hours ago. She needed help. Lucas needs help, and you're never around."

"I'm busy. They know that." He sniffled loudly. "I didn't come here to clean up. Looks like you're doing a fine job, whoever you are." He flicked his hair and shoved his hands in his pockets. "Tell Celeste I came by."

Before Filipe had time to respond, Hugo took the stairs and disappeared.

Filipe closed the door with a soft click and stood for a moment, thinking about the encounter. Was he going to tell Celeste? He'd have to ponder whether he could keep a neutral opinion when he told her instead of saying what he really thought of Hugo.

Filipe spent the next half hour cleaning up around the small space. The modest apartment had definitely seen better days, as he noticed the walls in need of a fresh coat of paint, the faucet in the bathroom with a slow leak, a burned spot on the Formica counter, and chipped tiles on the kitchen floor. He would feel more at ease if Celeste and Lucas lived in a better part of town and in a newer, nicer apartment. But what right did he have? Nothing more than that of a concerned friend when he longed to be so much more.

Before leaving, Filipe checked on Lucas and Celeste, who slept calmly and showed no signs of illness. His heart skipped a beat at the sight. He wanted them in his life—Celeste and Lucas. The conviction grew inside him. He wanted the right to help them, to live with them. The right to love them. And not just from afar, not only as a friend.

The thought stopped Filipe in his tracks. It came out of nowhere, but the more he rolled it around in his head, the more it made sense to him. There was nothing more he wanted. It was as simple as that. Only there was nothing simple about it, with so many things in the mix.

As much as he wished to stay tonight, he forced himself to turn around and go, locking the door before he left.

He could only hope Celeste would let him back in.

On Monday morning, Filipe sent a text to Celeste telling her to stay home and not worry about coming to work. She and Lucas needed the time to rest and recover.

As much as he wished to see them again, he could spend a day working on his list of tasks and focus on the business instead of his personal life.

After a quick breakfast at the hotel, Filipe walked the short distance to the aquarium. Despite the early hour, two cars sat in the front parking lot. He recognized one as belonging to Alice and was surprised she'd arrived so early on the first day of the week. Punctuality was not one of her qualities, as he'd come to learn. Maybe today he could take her aside and mention a few things that had been bothering him about her performance as the assistant director.

He found her on the east grounds, accompanying a man who carried a clipboard in his hands and a measuring tape clipped to his belt.

Was there something scheduled for today Filipe had forgotten about? His calendar was clear.

He approached them. "Good morning. I'm Filipe Romano, the owner. Is there something I can help you with?"

"Good morning, Filipe," Alice said. Whatever her goal was, her placid, almost pleasing expression had the opposite effect on him.

The man glanced at Filipe as he kept taking notes. "I'm Dr. Manuel Macedo, architect and head building and license inspector for the region."

Filipe frowned. "License and building inspector? What's going on?" He kept his voice calm. "Why wasn't I made aware of this visit?"

"No need to get defensive, Senhor Romano," the man said in a condescending voice. "A surprise inspection is never scheduled beforehand. It would defeat the purpose."

"Did you know about this?" Filipe asked Alice.

"Of course not," she replied quickly, her tone bordering on offended.

Her reaction didn't alleviate Filipe's concerns. Why had she arrived so early then? She never came on time. Her behavior had been less than professional on several occasions, and besides being late, she also left early sometimes. He wanted to ask her more questions but held back until the inspector left. It wouldn't look professional to have a discussion of this nature with one of his employees in front of someone who didn't work there.

The man finished writing and put his pen away. "I would like to see your building plans and licenses, including records of everyone working on this project."

"Certainly," Filipe replied. "Please come this way." He had nothing to hide. The faster he collaborated with this man's requests, the quicker he could get him on his way.

Alice followed them. As the assistant director, her presence was part of her duties, but Filipe couldn't ignore the feeling she had something to do with this surprise inspection. His instincts told him she was involved, and he planned to find out just how much she really was.

After retrieving all the pertinent paperwork, Filipe laid it out on the table in the workroom. "Building warrants for inside and outside, licenses and permits, and the plans for each zone of the project. And a list of workers from the contractor," he added.

"Thank you," Dr. Macedo said. He proceeded with his examination of each piece of paper and sheet, one by one, slowly and methodically, as if he had all the time in the world to carry this task to completion.

Filipe abhorred slowness in the workplace, unless warranted by safety, which was not the case. He pulled a chair and sat down at the other end of the table, then took his phone out and absently scrolled through Facebook, trying to keep his patience in check. There was nothing he could do to expedite the process, so he would sit and wait. He glanced at Alice, and she was also looking through her phone.

Exactly how long would this guy take to look through everything? Was there something specific he was looking for?

Forty minutes later, Dr. Macedo signed a form and detached it from his clipboard. He rose, and Filipe did as well, his legs protesting for the lack of activity.

"This is my preliminary report," Dr. Macedo said, gesturing at the piece of paper. "You'll receive the in-depth report within four business days, after which you may accept the fines or ask for an extension to correct the violations and a subsequent reevaluation." He walked toward the door.

"Violations?" Filipe grabbed the paper and scanned it. "What violations?"

Dr. Macedo paused and turned to Filipe. "For starters, lack of proper licensing for the temporary workers and the permit for land-disturbing activity, which doesn't include the grading near the pond."

"That doesn't make any sense," Filipe said. "All the licensing is up to date and the permits all inclusive." He had checked everything himself and with his contractor.

"As I said, my detailed report will have my findings itemized, and you will have a period to present evidence to corroborate your claims or accept the fines."

"What do you propose I do until then?"

"Nothing. This renovation is on hold until further notice. Also, don't forget to make sure your long-term employees are properly licensed and insured."

The situation was turning more and more bizarre with each passing minute. "What does that mean?" Filipe asked.

"It means I'll ask to see proof of licensing and insurance for all the employees associated with this premises, including the scientific specialists."

"What brought your attention to this project?" Filipe asked, curious to discover how the man had found out about the renovations at the aquarium. Had word gone out that Filipe was getting ready to put it on the market?

"A concerned citizen alerted the inspection office to the irregularities in this project," Dr. Macedo replied. "Good day." He exited the building calmly, in total contrast to what had just happened. He'd done the proverbial dropping of the bomb and then walked away from it.

Filipe now had to deal with the aftermath, hoping he could get everything back in order as soon as possible. He'd be losing money daily for each day the crew didn't work, not to mention the overall inconvenience. What a mess.

He sent a message to the contractor and the crew leader, asking to meet with them that morning. Then he asked Ross to call his lawyer and the architect. It was shaping up to be a long day.

Alice had followed Dr. Macedo to his car, and when she returned to the building, Filipe stopped her.

"Alice," Filipe said. "A word, please."

"Yes?"

"What do you know about this? The irregularities and violations mentioned."

"Nothing. He literally arrived a minute after I did," she replied. "He showed me his credentials, so I opened the gate for him."

"And you didn't think to call me?"

"I was going to when you showed up."

Whether she'd planned to call him or not, he couldn't know. "In the future, call me immediately if I'm not around. And today, stay until the end of your shift, please."

At first she didn't respond. "What about your head aquarist? Why isn't she here yet?"

"Celeste and her son are sick. I gave her the day off." Not that it was any of Alice's business.

"Special treatment is frowned upon," she said. "You should well know that."

"It's not special treatment. I'd do the same for any other employee." Filipe focused on her. "Why the less-than-friendly attitude toward Celeste? Is there anything going on I don't know about?"

"I don't have bad feelings toward anyone," Alice said, her voice contradicting her words. "I only wonder why Celeste holds a position of leadership when she fails to have a professional aquarist license."

Filipe's eyes flicked, despite his attempt to remain impassive. Was it true?

"You didn't know, did you?" Alice asked with a look of triumph, confirming Filipe's suspicions regarding the animosity she harbored against Celeste. "Senhor Xavier was in the process of firing Celeste for her lack of qualifications, but I couldn't find the paperwork after his death. I wouldn't be surprised if she found and got rid of it."

"That doesn't make any sense," Filipe said. "I've been using Senhor Xavier's office, and I haven't seen any signs of forced entry."

"As if getting access would be too hard for her," she scoffed.

"Meaning?"

A cold glint passed in her eyes. "It's common knowledge you and Celeste share a past acquaintance." Her tone bordered on malicious.

Filipe squared his shoulders. "Watch out what you say, Alice. What you're implying is a serious accusation."

She leaned in a fraction. "If I were you, I'd be more concerned with my relationship with a fraud."

As she turned and left, Filipe was too dumbfounded to say anything. The accusations toward Celeste were especially vicious. Was any of it true, and if it was, how did it have any bearing on Celeste's performance as a professional? The former director hadn't found it a problem, had he?

Filipe sighed in frustration. After such a great weekend, the new week was starting out decisively not great. And how was he going to deal with Alice? Even though he couldn't prove it, he was convinced she'd been the one to call the building inspection office. Disentangling the aquarium's renovation from this mess was going to take time he didn't have.

CHAPTER NINE

On Monday morning, Celeste woke with a sense something was amiss. She sat up in bed, and the memory of the previous night returned, when she and Lucas had been so sick.

She jumped out of bed and quickly turned to Lucas's bedroom to check on him. Had he needed her during the night? She couldn't even remember getting to her bedroom.

Lucas lay in his bed, a leg on top of the sheets. She touched her fingers to his forehead and found no trace of fever. Slowly, more memories crawled to the front of her mind. Lucas had puked all over himself and his bed, but the floor looked clean, the sheets had been changed, and Lucas smelled fresh and wore clean pajamas.

Filipe.

Hugo hadn't replied or shown up, but Filipe had called on the phone to find out why she'd left from

Porto without waiting for him, but she hadn't been in a condition to talk, let alone reply to what he sought. He'd offered to come when she told him they were sick, and she'd replied no, but he'd come anyway. Celeste remembered opening the door to him.

She padded to the kitchen. The dirty dishes had been washed and put away, the counters wiped, the floor swept. She walked through the rest of the apartment to see that Filipe had straightened the living room, cleaned the bathroom, taken out the full garbage bags, then replaced them with new, empty ones. He'd even put Lucas's sheets in the washer, which she quickly hung up on the line to dry.

In the refrigerator, she found the soup he'd brought. She poured the contents in a small pot to warm on the stove. Celeste sat at the kitchen table while she waited, overwhelmed and grateful. Her heart softened. When was the last time she'd had someone do anything for her and Lucas?

Hugo had never been the kind of husband to pitch in. Early on in their marriage, they'd slipped into more traditional roles, despite both of them having jobs. Even during her pregnancy and after Lucas was born, Hugo still hadn't helped, and even resented the time and attention she gave the baby.

After Hugo lost his job, he'd spent less and less time at home, until it came to the point that he was barely there, and finally she just asked him for a divorce. By then, they hadn't been a family of three for quite some time, and she was relieved when he'd agreed to it. She welcomed the change in status and only regretted the way it affected Lucas. Unfortunately, he never rose to the role of father she'd envisioned for Lucas, and nowadays Hugo was only too happy to allow Celeste to take his son on his weekend.

Celeste had been on her own for so long, she never even thought to ask for help, never expected it. And now she didn't know how to deal with what Filipe had done for them, for both her and Lucas. Notwithstanding the midnight kisses they'd exchanged on Saturday night, she knew Filipe was a friend and he cared for her.

She found her phone in her purse with a low battery. After plugging it in to charge, she scrolled through the notifications and found Filipe's latest text message.

Don't worry about coming to work today. Take the time to get better, you and Lucas. I'll check on you later.

The words filled the screen, and she stared at them, unable to think of a reply. A simple thank-you was not enough, but she had to start somewhere.

Thank you. For everything, she added.

Filipe's reply came immediately. **No problem. Are you and Lucas feeling better? Do you need anything?**

Lucas is still sleeping, but he looks fine. I'm feeling better too.

I'm glad. You two didn't look too good yesterday.

You didn't have to clean my apartment, Filipe.

I figured you could use a break.

He was right, of course. Celeste took a deep breath. **I'm sorry for leaving without telling you.**

147

Don't worry about it. We'll find another chance to talk.
Yes, I'd like that.
I'll talk to you later.

Celeste swiped at the screen and turned the phone to sleep mode face down on the table.

What kind of talk did he want to have? Did he mean to bring up the kiss? What would she say to that?

Here was Filipe back in her life, offering friendship and company, befriending her young son, and showing her the love and support that extended family could be—and she was struggling to know what to do with it.

Because she was afraid.

What she had was a plain and simple fear of being hurt and rejected and losing more than what she had before. And to complicate matters, there was too much unresolved about their past.

"Mamã?"

Lucas appeared at the door, his hair poking up in all directions. Celeste opened her arms, and he pressed his small body against hers, still warm and soft from bed and sleep. She kissed his cheeks while he let her. Sometimes, when he returned from spending time with his dad, he shrank from her and declared himself too old for cuddles and hugs. So she hugged him a little tighter when she could, taking advantage of his fresh-out-of-bed state and his willingness to return her embrace. He was growing too fast, and she wasn't ready for it.

At last he pulled back, and she let him go. "How are you feeling? Is your tummy better?"

Lucas nodded and patted his stomach. "I think the sick is gone from my belly. It's hungry again."

"It is? We'll have to feed that hungry belly, then." She poked a finger at this middle and he laughed.

They spent the rest of the morning inside, taking it easy like Filipe had suggested. Lucas had recovered well and was ready for his regular routine, asking her repeatedly to go to the aquarium to see the swans. Fearing a relapse, Celeste convinced him to stay in. They watched movies, built a fort of blankets under the kitchen table, and had a picnic on the living room floor of soup, saltwater crackers, and bananas, just in case regular food was too much.

By the end of the afternoon, Lucas's energy was boundless, and Celeste's patience was limited.

When Hugo's call came, asking to see Lucas for dinner, Celeste hesitated. Lately, it seemed he only brought drama into their lives, and she didn't want his negativity spilling into Lucas's mood. But he was the father, and denying him would be wrong.

He arrived on time—for a change—and waited by the front door while Lucas put on his shoes.

"Take it easy with him, please," Celeste said. "He was sick last night, and he might not be completely recovered."

"Is that guy here again?" Hugo asked with a glance toward the inside of the apartment.

"What guy?"

"Sounds like he didn't tell you I dropped by." His voice held a tone of accusation.

"You came by? When?"

"At the end of the day. Who's he?"

"Just a friend," she said. So much more than a friend, but not worth trying to explain to him. He'd never understand.

Lucas, as she'd expected, was overjoyed to leave with his dad and barely looked back when they left. She watched them from the living room window as they drove away, hoping Hugo would be on his best behavior. It was pathetic she had more faith in her five-year-old son than she did in her ex-husband.

She looked around, momentarily lost at being alone and with not much to do. Picking up in the living room and making the beds took only a few minutes. Filipe had been thorough with his cleaning on Sunday night.

As she glanced at her phone on the counter, a crazy idea flashed through her mind. Celeste grabbed it and typed a message to Filipe before she came to her senses.

Is spaghetti with meatballs still your favorite?

As soon as she hit send, a sense of panic coursed through her body. Too late to take it back. Was this what she wanted? To spend time alone with Filipe? They'd left things in limbo after the kiss last Saturday, and a conversation was due.

Depends on who's making it.

Celeste's mouth quirked at his reply. Still a picky

eater, after all this time.

I've learned a few things since I was seventeen, she replied.

I'm sure you have.

I meant cooking.

Of course. That's what we're talking about, right?

Come at seven. If you're not too busy.

Never too busy for you.

There he was, flirting with her again. Everything with Filipe seemed so easy and light when they texted. Until they met in person. Then, neither one of them knew how to treat the other. Unless she counted the one-time kiss.

One thing she knew—kissing Filipe one time had only made her realize how many more times she really wanted to kiss him.

Filipe knocked on the door and shifted the bag in his hands. He'd be lying to himself if he said he wasn't nervous. The last time he'd been here, Celeste and Lucas had been too sick, and the time before that, the invitation had come from the boy, despite Celeste's insistence he come.

But today she'd initiated it, both the text and the offer of dinner. And here he was, with sweaty palms and a rapid heartbeat, his body betraying the stern talking-to he'd had with himself before leaving—*take it easy.*

When she opened the door, Filipe stared, temporarily speechless. She was dressed simply in a fitted T-shirt and skinny jeans, both pieces showcasing her curves. At the sight of her bare feet, he swallowed.

A beeping sound came from somewhere inside, and she turned, looking over her shoulder. "Lock the door, will you? I need to drain the pasta."

He finally came to his senses and did as she asked, then followed her down the short hallway. Her hair was piled on top of her head, leaving her neck exposed, and Filipe forced himself to slow down. He'd always loved the sight of her neck, and the desire to reach an arm around her waist, pull her against his chest, and kiss her skin behind her ear—he'd be in trouble if he didn't keep himself in check.

In the kitchen, Celeste stood at the sink with a pot in her hands, draining the water.

Filipe walked to the refrigerator and stuck the ice cream carton inside the freezer. "I brought some ice cream. Lucas's favorite flavor."

She turned to him and smiled. "Sweet cream?"

Filipe nodded. "Where is the little guy?"

Celeste set a serving bowl on the table and winced. "Hugo took him out for dinner. Quite unexpectedly, I might say."

With Lucas gone, it was just him and her. Filipe's pulse jumped.

A blush stole across her cheeks, as she must have seen what he was thinking. Probably not too hard to guess.

The small kitchen didn't afford much room, and he was determined to give her space. Remembering how she'd felt in his arms and the way they'd kissed just last week had him wishing for more, but the memories would have to suffice. The guilt he'd been carrying for his part in her brother's accident was not the kind of thing to be overlooked in a relationship, and the last thing he wanted was to bring more pain to Celeste's life.

Celeste stepped behind the counter and opened a drawer. "Hugo mentioned you two met on Sunday night."

Filipe took a step back, as if physical distance between them could break the pull he felt, and leaned against the doorjamb. "He knocked on the door when I was straightening out a few things."

"How did that go?" Celeste raised her eyes at him from across the kitchen, then walked over with a serving fork.

"I might have been a bit too honest with my opinion," Filipe confessed.

She motioned for him to sit. "I'm not sure if I should be happy I missed it or sorry I wasn't there to watch it."

"Take my word. You didn't miss anything." Other than two men measuring each other up like cavemen.

The table was already set with two of everything, and he took the chair at the end like he had last time, only Lucas wasn't there to diffuse the tension that threatened to rise already.

At first, neither of them said much, concentrating on the food.

"This is really good," he said, raising his eyes at Celeste. "Thanks for inviting me."

Celeste smiled. "You're welcome. I'm glad you could come."

"I'm glad you and Lucas are feeling better," Filipe said.

She nodded. "That was not fun, but thank goodness it ran its course fast. How did the day go at the aquarium?"

Filipe placed his knife and fork down. "It started rather strangely with a surprise visit from a building and license inspector." He told her how he'd found Alice already on the grounds with the inspector and how the man had requested to see all the paperwork related to the renovation project.

"How odd," Celeste said. She got up, opened the fridge, and retrieved two stainless steel dessert cups. "I hope you don't mind chocolate mousse. I'll save the sweet cream ice cream for Lucas some other time." She handed him one along with a spoon.

"You remembered," Filipe said to her, momentarily distracted. Chocolate mousse had been his favorite dessert ever since he could remember, and she hadn't forgotten it either.

He took a bite, savoring the chilled, smooth texture and the rich, deep flavor of dark chocolate infused with a splash of espresso. Just the way he liked it.

He licked the spoon to the very end. "I haven't had mousse like this in years."

Celeste smiled, her eyes shining with what could only be a hint of pride and satisfaction.

Reluctantly, Filipe continued. "Do you remember the last time the former director had a surprise inspection?"

"In all the years I've been at the aquarium, not a single one," she replied.

Filipe frowned. "No inspections?"

"We had inspections but not surprise ones. They were always scheduled," Celeste confirmed.

"And since the director's death, have you had anyone come by?"

"We did, right after he died," Celeste said. "The inspection failed, and the aquarium was closed to guests."

"From what agency did the inspector come?" Filipe asked.

"The National Association for Regulation of Zoos and Aquariums."

Filipe leaned forward and rested his elbows on the table. "That makes more sense than having a building and license inspector drop by unannounced."

Celeste brought over two small cups with instant espresso. "Did he come on account of the renovation? What did he tell you?"

"He said a concerned citizen informed the office about the renovation, but I'm not buying it." Filipe stirred the coffee slowly.

"It sounds very convenient," Celeste said. "What did he even find to cite? You have everything in order."

Filipe smiled at her in gratitude. That was exactly the kind of support he needed, from a friend who knew him and knew he wouldn't try to be dishonest in his business dealings.

He related to her what the preliminary report said. "The inspector said the in-depth report will be available in four days."

"And in the meantime, you can't go on with the work. What did Alice say to all this?"

"She said she didn't know anything about it, but that I should watch out for—" Filipe rubbed the side of his neck, pondering the best way to bring up the subject.

Celeste raised an eyebrow. "Let me guess. She said something about me."

"She said you don't have an aquarist license," Filipe told her.

Her hesitation was minimal, but he caught it. "It's true, I don't. I didn't attend the last semester of classes." Her shoulders slumped in resignation. "Was that all she said?"

"I'm sorry I have to ask these questions," he said, hating himself for doing it.

Celeste waived her hand in a dismissal gesture. "I already know Alice doesn't like me. It can't be any worse than what she's told me to my face."

It didn't make any sense why Alice treated Celeste this way. "She said the director told her he was in the process of firing you."

Celeste's eyes widened. "No, that's not true. Why would he? I always passed the employee evaluations. We had a good professional relationship, and he was like a mentor to me. He would have told me face-to-face if there was something he didn't like about my work."

Filipe reached his hand and touched hers. "I believe you. Of course I believe you. I just wish there was a way of proving that Alice called to alert this new inspector."

"You think she's involved?"

"I have a gut feeling she is, but no proof, and I can't just let her go of without just cause." The rights of employees were a delicate subject. He'd have to meet with his lawyer and find out what he could do regarding the situation before he contemplated firing Alice. "I know I'm the owner now and I make the decisions, but I almost wish I could talk to Senhor Xavier and get his opinion," he confessed to Celeste.

Feeling like an outsider in his own business was foreign for him. He had a reputation for making sound decisions that had led him this far, and he always trusted his instincts. But now, with Celeste and Lucas in his life, it seemed his heart had taken over, instead of his mind, and he liked the way it made him feel, despite the roadblocks thrown at them.

Celeste moved to the sofa, and he followed.

"Too bad he didn't leave his planner to the next owner," she said, settling against the corner, her feet tucked under.

"What planner?"

"He had a small black leather planner he carried all the time, and he wrote notes on it when he was at work. I remember asking him about it one time, and he said he could run the aquarium with all the information in there."

"Do you know what happened to it?"

Celeste shook her head. "I packed up all of his belongings and sent them to his widow, but I don't remember seeing it." She reached for her phone and scrolled down the screen until she found the name she was looking for. "I could ask his wife if the planner ever showed up. I still have her phone number."

"That could be helpful," Filipe said. Maybe the planner didn't have anything in it, but it would be worth a try, if Celeste could find it.

Celeste watched him, a sort of expectation and hope in her expression that pulled at him like a magnet. He reached over and held her hand, and she leaned forward in his direction, gripping his with the same pressure.

Filipe moved closer to her. "How about we leave the business conversation for another day?"

A small smile tugged at the corner of her mouth, and her eyes softened. "What do you propose we talk about then? We still have some time before Lucas returns."

Filipe traced a slow circle with his thumb on the back of her hand. "We definitely should make good use of it. And not just with talk."

Celeste chuckled lightly even as a soft blush colored her cheeks.

"But first I need to tell you. I've been thinking a lot about what you told me on Saturday. Because I left right after Eduardo's accident, I didn't know a drunk driver caused it. I've been carrying this guilt"—he touched the middle of his chest—"for what I believed was my fault. I left you and tried to forget about you, about us. All these years, Celeste." Filipe swallowed hard, warring with so many emotions. "So much wasted time. I hope you can forgive me."

Celeste lifted a hand and touched the side of his face. "There's nothing to forgive."

Filipe caught her fingers and brushed her knuckles with his lips, then leaned in and kissed her. Gently. Fully. Completely.

When Celeste returned his kiss, his heart righted itself.

This was what he'd been missing for so long—Celeste in his life.

CHAPTER TEN

Filipe didn't sleep well. After talking with Celeste on Monday night—and kissing her thoroughly—he'd returned to his hotel room, where he spent all night wishing he didn't have to be apart from her. But the peace that came from being back in her life filled the hole that had plagued him for the past twelve years.

All this time, he'd effectively put Celeste and Eduardo in the back of his mind, squarely put away and covered up. Every year, on the anniversary of Eduardo's accident, he took the memories out for the day, dusted them off, gave them the proper thought and contrition, and then put them all back. It had been easy to do with Eduardo dead and Celeste gone.

But now he was ready to rebuild his life at her side, if she let him. He'd walked away from her once, but he wouldn't do it again.

When Wednesday morning first crawled into the night sky, Filipe rose from bed and made a cup of instant coffee from the side bar in his suite. He walked out on the balcony, then sipped the hot liquid slowly, wishing it could wake up more than just his tired brain after a restless night. The crisp air turned his skin into goose bumps, and he turned his face to the pale light.

A mix of anticipation and optimism had made its way into his chest, and the feeling was almost unfamiliar. He'd been wallowing in his own darkness for so long, the lightness and confidence were almost too much.

Filipe joined Ross for breakfast before walking to the aquarium. The meetings they'd had the day before with the lawyer and crew manager had gone well, but they still couldn't contest the inspection, or address the violations, until the full report was filed with the city bureau.

Ross brought him up to speed on the preparations and plans for the resort's reopening press conference, and Filipe took notes on his tablet. In the back of his mind, the evening spent with Celeste played like a movie on a loop, even as he tried to concentrate on the task at hand. Tuesday had been busier than normal and he hadn't had the time to see her. Texting with her had definitely not been enough.

"Have you come to a decision?" Ross asked.

"About?" Filipe scrolled through the page in front of him, trying to remember what he and Ross had been discussing.

"The aquarium," Ross replied. "I've seen you there every day with the construction team."

"Just getting it ready for the inspection. It won't sell without a renewed license."

"So you are going to sell, then?" Ross raised an eyebrow at him.

Filipe rubbed a spot on his temple. "I'm not sure anymore."

With very few exceptions, Filipe had always been able to make business decisions without involving his personal opinion. Well, almost always. He'd pulled out of the sale of Sunset Manor in Castelo Branco at the last minute. It hadn't felt right to sell it then. Having his cousin Catarina and her husband Afonso nearby to keep the manor and grounds in good condition had made the decision easier.

When he'd arrived from Angola, the aquarium had been like many other projects he'd had in recent years—something impersonal, if not a little inconvenient. But now it held a different interest since it mattered a great deal to Celeste and Lucas. How could he get rid of it knowing how they felt about it? He wanted to give them everything they wished for, and it wouldn't take too much to do it.

Maybe the surprise inspection was a blessing in disguise. With the renovation on hold, Filipe had more time to plan a reopening after the work was done instead of looking for buyers to offload it.

Ross eyed him and nodded slowly. "Are things all right?"

Filipe gave him a tight-lipped smile. "They'll be eventually."

Ross nodded again, and they returned to the schedule for a few more minutes.

When Filipe arrived at the employee building at the aquarium, Alice Vieira came out of her office to meet him.

"Filipe. I mean, Senhor Romano." She sent him a coy smile.

He ignored her slip and walked to the supply closet and retrieved a tool caddy. "What can I do for you, Dona Alice?"

Hopefully the formal names and tone would keep her in place.

She'd been trying to insinuate herself more and more each time she saw him at the aquarium with flirtatious comments and suggestive winks. Filipe had been ignoring it until now, but that didn't look like the right response anymore.

He didn't wait for her as he carried the caddy to one of the tanks.

"Please, call me Alice." She waited for a reply from him, but he didn't acknowledge her comment. She went on. "I have some ideas I'd like to discuss with you. About the aquarium," she added.

Filipe extended the measuring tape and wrote down the measurements on his phone. "Sure. We can schedule a meeting with António and the other keepers."

"I'm pretty sure we don't need to meet with all of them. You're the owner, and I'm the assistant director. What about we meet for dinner after hours?" Her suggestive look left no doubts as to what she really wanted.

Filipe straightened and looked at her. "How about I pretend I didn't hear that since it's against company policies?"

Her face turned red, and her expression soured. For a moment, she didn't say anything.

"I'll get the meeting scheduled," she replied at last. She started walking away but then returned. "By the way, I had to write up Celeste Ferreira this morning. She called to say she was taking her kid to the doctor, but since she hadn't asked for a sick day in advance, she's in violation of company policy regarding unauthorized days off."

Filipe frowned at her. "You wrote her up for taking care of her kid?"

Alice dropped a hand to her waist. "Well, company policies are to be upheld, right?" She turned her back on him and walked away.

Was she really that petty and without compassion?

"Dona Alice," he called back, and she paused. "I'd like to see the personnel records for all the aquarium's employees, including your own. As soon as possible, please."

She nodded. "Very well."

Filipe put down the measuring tape and blew a frustrated sigh. He should have looked at the employee files when he first arrived. But the work at the hotel had taken precedence and he'd believed he could trust the assistant director. It was obvious now she didn't deserve to be entrusted with personnel matters.

In the meantime, he'd talk to Ross about updating the internal policies on all levels and for all locations, including the aquarium. It would take some work and coordination with the local managers, but it was definitely necessary.

Before leaving, he took a long walk around the building, stopping to look more closely at each exhibit and tank.

When he arrived at the indoor bird enclosure, Luís and Dr. Abarca knelt on the floor inside examining the old swan.

"Dr. Abarca, is everything okay?" Filipe asked.

Dr. Abarca stood. "This old guy is not feeling well," he said. "I'm taking him to the clinic where I can watch him better." He walked over, removed his gloves, and shook Filipe's hand. "Call me Nuno, or I'll be forced to call you Senhor Romano."

Filipe returned the handshake. "Call me Filipe." He looked around but failed to see any kind of carrying crate. "How are you going to transport the swan?"

"Will you hand me that blue bag over there?" Nuno Abarca asked.

Filipe frowned. The only bag he could see was the iconic large bag from the Swedish ready-to-assemble furniture store. "This one?"

"That very one." Nuno took the bag and opened the gussets slowly until the bag stood by itself on the floor. Next he pulled out a fabric-like length of material from his pocket and a new pair of gloves, which he promptly put on.

"I'm guessing you've done this before," Filipe said.

Nuno nodded as he knelt again on the floor. "I've grown used to working with big birds when I come here. It's really not that hard. I just need to be careful not to spook him. First, I lift the legs above the tail and tie them back with an old pair of my wife's pantyhose." He went through the motions as he explained.

"Your wife?" Filipe asked, unable to hide his surprise.

Nuno paused momentarily and glanced at Filipe. "So that's where the hostility came from when we met before." He gave him a wry smile. "You thought I was interested in Celeste."

Filipe shrugged. "I wasn't hostile." He'd tried to hide his antagonism but apparently had not succeeded.

Nuno chuckled. "Sure. If you insist." He turned back to the swan. "We want to restrain him so he doesn't injure himself or others. Ready, Luís?"

The younger man nodded, and they each lifted the bird and placed him inside the bag. Next, Nuno placed a small blanket on the swan and crossed the bag's handles until the swan's back was covered. He gently lifted the swan's neck and cleared his head over the bag's opening at one end. Despite having only his head poking out, the swan appeared calm.

Nuno stood again and grabbed one handle. "Come on, Filipe. Help me out to my van." He gestured to the other handle.

Filipe walked over and took the other handle and then waited for Nuno's signal to lift.

"Not as heavy as I thought," Filipe commented as they walked out the building and to the driveway.

"This one has lost a bit of weight," Nuno agreed. "But we're going to nurse him back to health."

Luís walked on ahead and opened the back doors to the van, then climbed inside to help.

"We need to position him facing forward or backward so he can use his head and neck to counterbalance the effects of acceleration and braking," Nuno said.

Carefully, Filipe and Nuno lifted the bag onto an area with folded blankets, after which Nuno and Luís tucked old pillows and rolled blankets around the bag until they formed a stabilizing nest around it.

After checking the swan was comfortable, Nuno thanked Luís, who exited the van and left.

Filipe couldn't pass up this chance to talk to Nuno "Do you mind if I ask you what you think of the aquarium?"

Nuno gently closed the van. "I heard a rumor you're selling."

"I haven't decided," Filipe replied. "My advisers told me to sell, but there's a couple of people I know who'll be really disappointed with me if I do."

"Celeste and her son," Nuno said. "Sounds to me that you know what to do."

Filipe slipped his hands in his pockets. Maybe the veterinarian was right and the decision was easier than he gave it credit. "Other than the aquariums in Lisbon and Porto, do you know of other small operations in the country?"

Nuno walked to the driver's side door and swung it open. "Not like this one. I'm from the area, and I remember when this place was new. With a little bit of time and effort, you could bring it back to its former glory." He shook Filipe's hand before entering the van.

Filipe watched him leave, thinking how much sense his words made. Maybe it was time he had the marketing team come up with a different plan for this place.

Once in his office at the hotel, Filipe pulled out his phone and sent a text to Celeste.

I heard Lucas isn't feeling well and you're taking him to the doctor. Disregard what Alice Vieira said. Take the day off. Take tomorrow off, too, if you need it.

The phone vibrated in his pocket as he sat down at his desk.

Are you sure? I don't want to create any problems.

I'm sure. How is he doing?

He had a high fever early this morning. We're at the dr. right now.

Keep me posted, and let me know if you need anything.

Thanks, Filipe.

Would she let him know? Maybe he'd check with her later.

His phone rang in his hand. It was Ross. "What's up?"

"You better meet me in the lobby. Right now, if you can."

Ross was never dramatic. The fact that his voice wavered at the last word only indicated something serious was amiss.

"I'm on my way," Filipe said.

He couldn't even begin to guess what the problem could be.

Celeste parked her car in the employee lot and walked to the side gate. Her car wasn't the first there, and she still had five minutes before clocking in on time. She'd been gone from work for two days this week. Lucas had returned sick after his outing with Hugo, and on top of the sickness he'd had after coming home from Porto, his little body had needed some medication and time to rest. Staying home with him one more day was out of the question, as she'd used all of her sick days for the quarter already.

Despite knowing he was in good hands, they were not her hands, and she worried about him. It didn't seem fair at times—having to split her attention and loyalty between her son and her job. How could she choose? Guilt rose again. At least she should be thankful she had a job she loved that paid the best she could get in this kind of position and with her unfinished degree. As for Lucas, he wasn't seriously ill; it was just a spring cold aggravated by a weak immune system from their bout with the stomach flu last week. He'd probably be feeling better by the time she picked him up.

Would she get to see Filipe today? With Lucas being sick again on Tuesday, she hadn't seen Filipe since Monday night when he'd come over for dinner. The hotel's grand reopening was approaching soon and with the license inspection unresolved and the renovation crew still gone, he might not come around to the aquarium. She missed him fiercely. The few texts they'd exchanged since the night he'd come over for dinner weren't enough—she longed to see him, hug him, kiss him. Tell him how she truly felt about him.

Celeste sighed. It would have to wait.

Her phone rang, and she stopped. The number was familiar but it didn't have a caller ID assigned to it. "Hello?"

"Is this Celeste Ferreira?" an older woman asked.

"Yes, this is her."

"This is Vitória Xavier. You left a message for me."

Vitória was Senhor Xavier's widow. Celeste had left a message asking if she could come by. "Dona Vitória, thank you for returning my call."

Through her years of working at the aquarium, Celeste had met Senhor Xavier's wife on a few occasions. They hadn't interacted much, but Celeste had hoped the old lady remembered her.

"Of course, dear. What can I do for you?"

"This might sound strange, but I'm wondering if you still have your husband's notebook, the one he kept for the matters related to the aquarium." Celeste paused. "I'd like to come see it, if that's possible."

"Yes, absolutely. Would you like to come later today?"

Celeste hadn't expected to be invited so soon, but if she worked through lunch, she'd be able to visit Vitória Xavier before picking up Lucas from daycare. "Today would be wonderful."

They settled on a time, and Dona Vitória gave Celeste her address and instructions on how to get there.

She pocketed her phone and turned her attention back to work and the feeding schedule at the aquarium.

It was rotation day. Heitor, Luís, and Marco had already arrived at the galley, and she greeted them. "Bom dia, senhores."

They returned the greeting, and she put the map and schedule down on the stainless steel counter. All of them wore long white aprons over the aquarium's employee T-shirts and white rubber boots. It was a uniform of sorts, at least on feeding days. The diets had been readjusted and posted the weekend before, including Dr. Abarca's suggestions for the animals and fish who needed special care. Part of the prep work was already finished and the food lay either in the freezer or in the refrigerator. Celeste and the other keepers had only the fresh fruits and vegetables to chop today.

Alice poked her head in midmorning, pinning a curious gaze at everyone. Her gaze landed on Celeste.

Celeste pulled away from the counter to wash her hands, but Alice waved her off.

"No need to do that," Alice said. "Please come see me before you leave at the end of the day."

"I'll be there," Celeste replied.

What could it be this time? Was she in trouble for the days she'd stayed at home with Lucas? Filipe had said not to worry about it, and while he was the owner, Alice was her immediate superior. One more concern to think about.

Among the four of them, the work progressed fast, and by lunchtime, they were done with all the food preparation and distribution. Feeding time was next, her favorite part of diet and feeding day. They split into two teams of two, pushing the carts and checking the diet plans for each animal and fish. She lingered on her favorites, like the ten-year-old tortoise who'd never grown as large as its enclosure mates. Sometimes Celeste felt the same, like she was perpetually trying to catch up to the demands of everyday life and not doing a very good job of it. Always behind.

In the pond, the female swan Bete looked a bit forlorn, probably missing her mate, something Celeste could easily relate to. Not that she had a mate, but there was someone she wouldn't mind filling the role. When had her life started imitating the animals' lives?

Afterward, she wrote down her observations, posted them where the other keepers could see, and walked down to the small office. Once there, she typed the information into the shared folders of the aquarium's main computer system, distractedly copying the notes and numbers from her clipboard.

Celeste worked through lunch, then sent a text to Lucas's daycare provider, who confirmed Lucas was doing well. Thank goodness for small miracles. Celeste breathed out a sigh of relief when she read the words on the screen.

By the time she knocked on Alice's office door, Celeste's workday had thirty minutes left, and she was looking forward to leaving. Hopefully whatever Alice wanted wouldn't take too long.

Alice sat at her desk, holding an open folder. "Take a seat," she said.

Celeste took a chair and waited for Alice to say something, as she had no idea what had brought her there.

After a few moments, Alice put down the folder. "Did you know there's a company policy against fraternizing among employees of the SoliMar Resort?"

Celeste's neck and cheeks heated. "Is this about the time I've been spending with Filipe Romano?"

Alice's eyes widened. "So you don't deny it?"

"Of course I don't deny it. Filipe was my brother's best friend when we were teenagers. We reconnected recently."

"This goes beyond an old family friendship, as you call it. I've been observing you these past few weeks, and you've been taking advantage of this connection in your favor."

Celeste straightened and tried to keep her voice steady. "Have you been following me?"

"No need for that. You were in public, after all. You've also brought your son to meet Filipe Romano, which furthers—"

"My son is five years old. He's a child. And I'm certainly not using him to further anything or take advantage of anyone." Celeste took a breath and slowed down her words. "As I said, Filipe Romano and I were friends a long time ago, but that hardly matters to what you're accusing me of. Without any foundation, I might add. I'm certainly not taking advantage of him or our past relationship to further my position at the aquarium."

This conversation was the most bizarre she'd ever had with anyone, not to mention utterly and completely removed from a professional tone. Why was she discussing her friendship with Filipe to a woman who clearly antagonized her? It didn't help any that Alice was Celeste's boss.

Alice tapped her pen. "It's not a past relationship. You have feelings for Filipe Romano. Why don't you just admit it already? You love him. Say it; say you love him."

Celeste took a breath and kept her calm. She wouldn't be admitting anything to Alice, who was clearly intent on rousing a reaction from her. Yes, Celeste loved Filipe, but he would be the first person she told, not this spiteful woman.

At the lack of reply from Celeste, Alice narrowed her eyes. "Your silence is enough admittance for me. As assistant director, I find you to be in violation of an internal policy that prohibits any relationships of a personal nature." She picked up the folder and opened it flat on the table. It was Celeste's employee records. "And after reviewing your information, which Senhor Romano asked me to, I discovered your qualifications don't meet the job requirement. You never finished your degree, a fact that Senhor Xavier was quite adept at keeping to himself."

Celeste had never lied or withheld information about her incomplete degree. Senhor Xavier had always known and had even encouraged her to go back to university and finish it, but she never quite got to it.

She stood her ground, guessing where the conversation was turning and hanging on to a last shred of serenity. Maybe it was the last thing she had, but she'd hold on to her professional demeanor.

Alice leaned back in her chair, calm and collected, as if she hadn't raised her voice less than a minute ago.

"The official announcement hasn't been made, but you'll be the first one to know that Senhor Romano promoted me to the position of aquarium director just this morning. And my first order of business is to relieve you of your duties. You're fired."

Celeste remained silent. What could she say to that? She didn't believe Filipe had kept such news from her, but she'd been too distracted to discuss the future of the aquarium with him. Whatever he'd decided, Celeste wasn't qualified for it. And now she was fired.

A strange calm filled her chest. Maybe later, the stark truth of what had just happen would hit her hard. But for now the shock hadn't arrived yet—just an eerie stillness and resignation at being let go from a job she not only needed but also loved.

She nodded curtly and left.

"Don't forget to leave your badge and keys," Alice added.

Celeste kept walking toward the employee building, glad she didn't encounter anyone on the way there and that the main room was empty when she arrived. She retrieved her purse from the bottom drawer of her desk and placed the badge and keys on top. After finding a reusable bag, she placed her few belongings inside, relieved she wouldn't have to return and see Alice again.

She wasn't surprised at this turn of events. Not at all. Alice's behavior and animosity toward Celeste had been building incrementally since Senhor Xavier's passing, and she'd finally acted on it and fired Celeste, even without a valid reason to do it.

When she arrived at her car, she placed the small box in the back seat and let her shoulders slump. The meeting with Alice had sapped all her energy, mental and physical, but she wasn't done for the day. She picked up her phone, opened the map application, and set a course to Dona Vitória's address. Maybe Senhor Xavier's notebook didn't have any answers, or maybe it didn't even exist anymore, but if she could find it and help Filipe, she had to give it a good try.

Dona Vitória lived in Peniche and despite the end-of-day traffic, Celeste arrived quickly.

When she arrived, the old lady opened the door and smiled wide. "Come in, come in. I'm so glad you came."

"Thank you." Celeste wiped her feet on the door-mat and stepped into the hallway.

Dona Vitória air-kissed Celeste's cheeks and ushered her to the front parlor. "I was so happy to hear from you."

She indicated a stuffed chair, and Celeste sat at the edge. "I'm hoping you might be able to help."

Dona Vitória took the sofa and pursed her lips. "At the risk of sounding really bizarre, I have to tell you something."

Celeste leaned forward. It couldn't be any worse than the day she'd had already, could it?

"I had the same dream with my husband this month. That's not the bizarre part," she hurried on to say. "I dream of him all the time, but those dreams are more like memories of moments we shared. This dream was different, more like he was sending me a message." The corner of her mouth pulled into a nervous smile.

Celeste leaned forward. "What type of message?"

The old lady's expression relaxed. "You don't think it's weird?"

"I lost my mother when I was eighteen, and I've had similar experiences, dreams that felt more purposeful and special than the average one." She still did at times.

Dona Vitória went on, as if encouraged by Celeste's reassuring reaction. "In the dream, António was writing at this desk. I couldn't see what he was writing, but in the third dream, he got up with this notebook and put it away in a box tucked in a lower cupboard. When I woke up, I went to the place and found the same notebook he had."

She rose and walked over to a shelf, retrieved something, then walked back to the sofa, where she sat back down. "I found it last wee,k and I've been trying to figure out what to do with it." She handed it to Celeste.

"This is the one he always wrote in at work," Celeste said, recognizing the notebook. "I need to show it to the new owner, but I'll get it back to you after."

"I hope it has what you need," Dona Vitória said.

"So do I," Celeste said.

Was she placing too much hope in it? What if it had the answers Filipe needed?

CHAPTER ELEVEN

Filipe stepped out of the shower and checked his phone once more. He still hadn't heard back from Celeste. His messages to her had gone unanswered on Wednesday, and the calls had the same result. He finally found some time to breathe and now he couldn't find her.

How many hours had he slept? Probably not as many as he needed. Despite a vigorous scrubbing, the smell of smoke persisted. Whether real or still ingrained in his brain, he couldn't tell.

He took a towel and rubbed his hair dry, then passed a hand over his chin. He hadn't shaved in two days, but spending precious minutes in front of the mirror instead of finding Celeste didn't appeal to him. Besides, wasn't the three-day scruff look in fashion right now? He'd blend right in.

In the closet, Filipe found a stark white button shirt and put it on, his mind wandering to the craziness of yesterday's incident.

The fire had started at the back of the parking lot, where the electrical charging stations were located. For reasons yet unknown, one of the stations had broken into flames that quickly spread to a vehicle charging.

Fortunately, nobody else was around the area at the time and there were no injuries. The car was a total loss, as were the five charging units, and the parking lot would have to be repaved in that area. Considering how fast it all happened, those were minor inconveniences he could live with.

Once the firemen put out the fire, and the police arrived, it had taken a while to get the bureaucracy of the incident sorted and the report done. The insurance adjuster had shown up a few of hours later, and by the time Filipe dropped into bed, he'd been exhausted. Ross would take care of containing the media this morning, even if Filipe still had to go in front of the cameras for a brief press conference. It was better to take charge from the beginning and control what was being said than wait for the media to put their own spin on things. That never worked well, and sometimes it even backfired. Filipe groaned. Wrong word there. He'd better think of what he was going to say first.

He didn't hear back from Celeste all morning. By lunchtime the tow truck had come to take away the burned car, the electric chargers had been removed by the manufacturing company, and the burned lot had been cordoned off. Filipe checked in with Ross, and since nothing else required his attention, he walked over to the aquarium.

Part of the construction team had returned and were busy removing some of the equipment they needed for another job. Filipe's lawyer was still working on clearing the violations, and soon the architect would have a new plan for a complete renovation with the intent to reopen to the public. Filipe waved at the workers as he made his way to the main building.

His mouth twitched in a small smile. He could imagine Celeste and Lucas's reaction when he told them of the news. Just thinking of their joy warmed his heart.

Celeste was nowhere to be found at the aquarium, and when he asked the other keepers, none of them had seen her since the day before. Where was she?

Alice Vieira walked out of her office as he passed by, and he braced himself for another awkward exchange.

But she didn't step uncomfortably close like last time. "Senhor Romano, how are you today? Everything all right? I heard about the fire in the hotel's parking lot."

Filipe stopped. "Yes, everything's fine now. No injuries, and the fire didn't spread past the parking lot."

"Thank goodness," she said. "It could have been a tragedy."

"I'm looking for Celeste Ferreira. Have you seen her today?"

For a moment, her face turned into a shrewd expression, but she quickly replaced it with a more neutral look. "She's no longer working at the aquarium. I found her keys and badge on her desk with a note saying she left."

Filipe's heart skipped a beat. "Left? What do you mean?"

She shrugged. "I mean she's gone. That's all I know. Did you have a question I can help with?"

A cold shiver ran through him. "No, thanks." He turned to leave, anxious to find Celeste and know what was going on.

"I got that meeting scheduled like you asked," Alice Vieira said after him.

"Send the details to my email," Filipe said over his shoulder. He had to get out of there as soon as possible.

Why was Celeste gone? Where was she, and why hadn't she called him?

Filipe pulled out his phone and tried her number again, frustrated when it went straight to voice mail.

His thoughts tumbled in his mind as he hurried to his underground private parking space and got into his car. He needed time to think away from the hotel and the aquarium.

Why had she left? It didn't make any sense.

Filipe drove out of the resort and headed south along the coast with the windows down and the breeze blowing his hair. He took the exit to the national road, anticipating the traffic on the freeway as the end of day approached and not caring that the alternative route took longer to get somewhere.

After a few minutes on the road, he made his way closer to the beach until he found a place to park. Filipe exited and leaned against the hood of the car, watching the water.

Despite the clear sky, the waves churned over themselves as they crashed on the surf. He was the same as the rough sea, smashing over and over into himself, trying to make sense of Celeste's departure.

The irony wasn't lost on him. Whether purposefully or not, she'd done to him what he'd done to her so many years ago, and Filipe couldn't blame her for it. He only wanted to know why and, once they talked, hopefully convince her to stay, to tell her how he felt and help her see how good they could be together.

He stayed awhile, yearning to lose himself and forget his responsibilities, wishing he had a wetsuit and board with him right then. Maybe that wasn't a good idea. The way his despondency distracted him, keeping himself firmly planted on land was a better alternative.

As the sun plunged into the ocean in the early evening, Filipe drove back to the SoliMar, resigned to Celeste being gone for now and already planning to go to her apartment.

When he drove by the aquarium on the way to the hotel, a group of people walked around the perimeter, and a few extra cars lined up at the visitor's parking. After parking back in his private spot, he took the service stairs to the lobby.

Ross stood at the check-in desk in front of a large tablet, a deep frown creasing his forehead.

"What's going on at the aquarium?" Filipe asked.

Ross jumped up from his seat. "Where have you been? I've been trying to call you for the past thirty minutes."

Filipe reached in his pocket and drew his phone out. The screen was black. "Looks like the battery died."

Ross approached Filipe and placed a hand on his arm. "Why do you have a car with a built-in charger if you keep forgetting the cord?" He steered them out of the room and across the lobby. "Come on, the boy is missing. We've been looking for him at the aquarium and just barely called the police. They should be here any minute."

"What boy is missing?"

"The head keeper's. Celeste Ferreira's son."

The shock passed through him like a bucket of cold water. He stopped. "Lucas is missing?"

Ross continued on, then returned to pull Filipe along with him. "I think that's his name. His mother is out of her mind."

Filipe didn't wait for the rest. He took off running in the direction of the aquarium, past the road and the approaching police cars, past the gate and the people milling around, until he saw Celeste standing by the door of the main building.

As soon as she noticed him, she set off in his direction. Filipe opened his arms, and she ran the rest of the way until they met in the middle, tightening their embrace around each other.

"He's gone, Filipe. I can't find him," she said against his chest.

He pulled away from her, took her hand, and grasped it tightly. "What happened?"

"I picked him up from daycare and told him we were driving straight to the hotel to give you the notebook instead of going home. But when we arrived he insisted on stopping here to see the swans, which were not outside. He got upset when I told him I didn't have the keys and we couldn't go inside." She took a deep breath and squeezed her eyes shut for a moment. "He ran away from me and hid behind the building, and when I went after him, he was gone."

"How long has he been missing?"

"Not even a half hour yet." She grimaced. "I should have prepared him better about this being my last time at the aquarium."

They sprinted toward the main gate, where the policemen had just arrived.

"Alice told me you left." He held on to her hands, afraid to let go of her.

Celeste slowed down at his side. "I didn't leave. I was fired because I'm unqualified and I love you."

Filipe glanced at her, unsure he'd heard her correctly. Given her emotional state, maybe she hadn't even realized what she'd said to him. As much as he wanted to know, this wasn't the time. Finding Lucas came first.

A plainclothes detective approached them. "Dona Celeste, what can you tell me about your son's state of mind the last time you saw him?"

Celeste's shoulders slumped. "He kept asking about the swan that left, and he was upset that I didn't have a key and badge to access employee buildings." She pulled out her phone and brought up a photo of Lucas on the screen. "This is the most recent photo I have."

The officer motioned over a uniformed policeman, who took Celeste's phone and left with it. Another policeman approached the detective, and they conferred for a minute.

"We're going to bring the dogs in," the detective said. "Do you have a piece of clothing he's worn recently?"

"I might have something in the car," Celeste replied as she walked toward the parking lot with the policeman beside her.

Filipe watched her go, wishing he knew where Lucas was to bring him home, watching the policemen walk around the perimeter calling out his name.

"What about the hotel?" he asked the younger officer. "Have they searched in the hotel yet?"

The policeman relayed the question into the radio. After waiting for the answer, he said, "Only outside."

Filipe set off at a brisk pace, intent on finding Lucas and delivering him to Celeste safe and sound. If this was partly about the swans, like it seemed it was, there was one place he could think of where Lucas might have gone, and Filipe had to give it a try.

When he arrived at the hotel, he crossed the lobby past the entrance and kept going to the small back room with shelves along two walls and several stuffed chairs in the center. At the farthest end, a round table with a decorative skirt was tucked between the window and the shelf. On top sat a library lamp that had been turned on and pushed to the edge, and to the side, facing the window, at an angle not visible from the door, the skirt had been hiked up as if it were the flap of a makeshift tent.

Underneath the table, lying on his belly, Lucas slept on top of the magazine article about swans, with his head resting on the crook of his elbow.

Filipe sat on the floor next to the sleeping boy and gently touched his arm. "Hey, Lucas."

After he called his name twice, Lucas rolled to the side and stretched. He yawned and slowly opened his eyes. "Hi, Filipe," he said in a sleepy voice. "What are you doing here?"

Filipe's tension eased out and he smiled. "I should ask you the same thing, buddy. What brought you here?"

Lucas slipped out from under the table into a seating position, and pulled the magazine onto his lap.

"My mom said we were leaving, so I had to come get this magazine. You said I could have it."

"You're right, I did say you could have it. I'm sorry I forgot to bring it to you."

"That's okay. I got it now."

"You gave your mom a scare, taking off without telling her."

Lucas's shoulders slumped. "I wanted the magazine," he said again. "We couldn't get inside to see the swans. Is she mad?" His voice lowered at the question.

"No, she's not mad. How about we go see her so she can stop worrying about you?" Filipe stood and extended his hand.

Lucas clutched the magazine to his chest, then grabbed Filipe's fingers with his free hand and pulled to a standing position. "That's a good idea. My mom worries a lot."

Filipe's mouth twitched in amusement as they exited the small library. "I bet she does."

Lucas nodded and looked up at Filipe. "She said she was worried about you."

Filipe met Lucas's gaze. "We can't have that, can we?"

At the sight of Lucas holding on to Filipe's hand in the hotel lobby, Celeste brought a hand to her mouth, and tears gathered at the corners of her eyes. A wave of relief swam through her. She ran to them and knelt in front of Lucas, gathering him in her arms.

"I came to get the magazine, and I fell asleep. I'm sorry, Mamã," Lucas said. "It's about swans." He pulled back a little and held up a crinkled magazine from between them.

"I'm just glad you're okay, Lucas." She kissed his cheeks.

After another hug, Celeste stood and grabbed Lucas's hand, then turned to Filipe and put her arm around his waist. "Thank you," she said, her voice choking with emotion.

Filipe returned the hug and whispered in her ear. "He's all right. Take a breath now." He guided her and Lucas to a nearby sofa, and she sat, pulling Lucas onto her lap, determined to never let go of him again.

Lucas raised a hand and touched her face. "Are you crying because of me?"

"They're happy tears, baby. I'm glad to have you back. That's all. Why don't you show me your magazine?"

Lucas opened the pages across their laps. "It has lots of nice pictures about swans. Black and white ones, and some are gray. See?"

From the corner of her eye, she noticed Filipe talking to the detective. They looked in her direction a few times but didn't approach. After a few minutes, the detective shook Filipe's hand and left.

Filipe walked over to them. "Let's go up to my suite before this gets out to the media."

"Do we need to go to the police station tomorrow?" sShe asked Filipe.

"No, it's all done. If anything else comes up, I'll ask Ross to take care of it."

Celeste followed, relieved she didn't have to deal with anything else at the moment. Everything else could wait.

When they arrived at Filipe's suite, Lucas let go of her hand and ran inside. The suite opened to a wide living room and small kitchen area, all decorated in white and blue with a large yellow sofa in front of a flat-screen television and a dining table by the balcony that faced the beach. In the morning the view would be quite spectacular.

"Your house is so big," he said to Filipe. "Can I watch TV?"

Filipe chuckled. "If it's okay with your mom."

"That's fine," Celeste said. Lucas was past his regular bedtime, but after the last two hours, she didn't care as much about enforcing rules as she did on other days. They'd earned a reprieve.

Lucas ran to the sofa and jumped on it. Filipe picked up the remote control and switched on the wide screen to a cartoon channel, looking to Celeste to check with her first. She nodded at him and made her way to one of the straight-backed chairs at the narrow island, just content to watch them. Her hands were cold, and she clasped them.

Her heart was slowly returning to its normal beat, and the tight band in her chest had loosened its hold on her heart. All the what-ifs flashed through her mind, but she didn't want to linger there and pushed them all away. It had barely lasted two hours from the time Lucas had run away from her until Filipe brought him to her—the longest hours of her life. If she lived to be one hundred, Celeste never wanted to go through that kind of anguish again.

Filipe sat by her. "I'm going to order dinner. What would you and Lucas like?"

"I want pizza," Lucas piped up from his seat on the sofa with a grin on his face.

Celeste smiled. "Of course you do. As long as you eat some salad with it," she added.

"Got it. Pizza and veggies." Filipe dialed a number on his phone, and half an hour later a knock sounded at the door. After tipping a young guy, he rolled in a food cart full of covered dishes.

Celeste rose, eager for something to do to occupy her hands. Along with three kinds of pizza and fresh-cut veggies, there was a covered dish with white rice, grilled chicken tenders, and a platter of thick-cut potato fries.

She took a slice of olive pizza onto a plate for Lucas and added sliced tomatoes and cucumbers. "How did you get all this done so fast?"

"I called the hotel chef. He's getting things ready for next week's grand opening," Filipe said.

Filipe sat on the floor with Lucas, and they ate at the coffee table in front of the sofa. Celeste loaded a plate with some fries and cucumbers and sat on a stuffed chair by them, pecking at the food. The interaction between Lucas and Filipe as they ate and commented on the animal show on the screen warmed her heart, a small smile pulling at the corner of her lips.

It was a domestic scene, a family vignette at dinnertime—mother, father, and son enjoying one another's company, like so many families did. Only they were not a family, and Filipe was not the father. Or husband. She sighed.

When Lucas fell asleep, Filipe carried him to the bedroom. Celeste went on ahead, drew the sheets back, and removed Lucas's shoes. She covered him with a sheet and bent to kiss his forehead.

Once in the living room, she picked up the plates and stacked them on the cart. She'd been planning to talk to Filipe—why was she so nervous now?

She moved to the sofa, and they sat close enough for their knees to touch.

"I went to see Dona Vitória, Senhor Xavier's widow, and got his notebook," she said. "With everything that happened with Lucas, I didn't have the time to look through it, but I have a feeling you'll find some answers in it. I'll get it for you tomorrow. It's in the car."

"Even if I don't find what I need, there will be some changes at the aquarium. It's about time I act like the owner I am and hire staff I can trust." Filipe reached for her hand. "I was waiting to do a grand gesture to surprise you and Lucas, but I might as well tell you I've decided to reopen the aquarium to the public."

Her heart jumped, and she threw her arms around his neck for a quick hug. "Thank you, thank you," she said, tears emerging again. "You won't regret it, Filipe. I know your advisers said it's not financially sound, but if there's anyone who can turn that around it's you." The conviction of her own words warmed her chest. "I can't wait to tell Lucas. He'll be so happy."

Filipe nodded, smiling. "Will you stay the night?" Filipe asked. "You can sleep with Lucas. It's a big bed. I can take the sofa, or I'll go to the room next door, if you're more comfortable with that."

"Don't go." She didn't want him to leave. "I'll stay with Lucas in the bedroom, if that's okay with you. I don't want to drive back home tonight." Her apartment was only thirty minutes away, but she wanted to stay. Here, next to him, she felt safe, for her and Lucas, and that was a feeling she didn't want to let go of.

Filipe took her hand, and she met his eyes, full of hope and alight with anticipation. Surely hers were a mirror of his, anxious as she was to tell him how she felt and what she hoped for.

"What you said earlier—is it true?" Filipe asked.

He had noticed her words after all. "This is so not how I planned to tell you." The nerves rose again, and she inhaled deeply for courage. "But yesterday Alice called me to her office and accused me of spending too much time with you, taking advantage of our connection, and breaking a company policy for it. She said I had feelings for you and challenged me to admit them. I didn't admit anything to her, but she fired me anyway."

Filipe groaned. "First, she can't fire you. I own the aquarium. Second—let me get this straight. You risked the job you love for saying—" he hesitated.

"For saying I lo—"

Filipe stopped her and placed two of his fingers on her lips. "Wait. You need to listen before you go on."

Celeste captured his hand and held it in hers, giving his fingers a squeeze, wanting him to know whatever it was he struggled with, it would be all right.

"I left after Eduardo's funeral twelve years ago because I didn't have the courage to face you. If only I'd gone with Eduardo that night, he might still be alive today. How could I have stayed and tried to have a chance at love with my best friend's little sister after letting him die?" He shook his head, a sadness dimming his expression. "I couldn't. I'd failed him, and I had failed you, and I certainly didn't deserve to be happy."

Celeste waited, hanging on to her patience as everything inside her screamed to tell him he was wrong. So wrong.

"But now, so help me." He took a deep breath and squeezed his eyes. "I'm not that young, self-sacrificing guy anymore. I want to be selfish, and I want to beg your forgiveness. Because I love you, Celeste, and I'll wait until you're ready."

"I don't want to wait." Celeste sat up straight, placed her hands on his shoulders, and kissed Filipe on the lips.

The familiar sense of coming home returned as she moved her lips against his.

His initial surprise quickly changed to complete participation, and Celeste's heart melted at the heat between them. He took over the kiss, moving from the exploration she started to an assuredness that was new, yet familiar. He grabbed her by the waist and brought her flush against him, and Celeste wound her arms around his neck, erasing whatever distance remained between them.

There was no hesitation between them, no probing, no questioning. The firmness and affirmation from Filipe matched her own, and her heart beat a new rhythm. Celeste unclasped her hands and touched his face, then brought her palms to rest on his chest, feeling his heart beat in time with hers. The solidity of his body beneath her hands, his scent, his skin—the feelings and sensations exploded within her, surpassing any expectations she'd ever entertained.

This was Filipe, the man she'd fallen in love with at fifteen, whom she loved so much more now than she had back then. Yet he was not the same man from back then, and neither was she the same girl he'd left behind. What she felt for him now was much, much stronger.

Filipe pulled away from her mouth, and she groaned in protest, but the separation barely lasted as he angled his face and kissed her neck, then the hollow of her throat, and a new wave of sensations followed.

"Celeste." His voice was thick with emotion as he pulled back to look at her intently. "I love you," he repeated. "Please tell me there's a chance for us."

"I love you too," she said. "I want this chance as much as you do. We'll make it work." She didn't know how yet, but she knew they would.

Filipe closed his eyes and let out a shuddering breath so full of emotion and relief, Celeste's chest heated at the feeling. He buried his face in her neck and inhaled deeply, tightening his hold on her. The embrace became as intimate as the kisses they'd just shared, and Celeste marveled at the closeness between them.

Even as they eased away from each other to breathe, Celeste wrapped her arms around his waist, and Filipe nestled her to his side and kissed her temple.

She looked up at him, and he smiled. "Celeste," he said. His voice hadn't yet recovered its steadiness, and she recognized the same emotion in herself.

"I love you," she repeated with firm eyes and as much conviction as she could muster. "I don't think I've ever stopped loving you."

A slow smile appeared in his face, and his eyes crinkled at the corners. "I love you too. I always have, and I always will."

Then he bent and kissed her again.

CHAPTER TWELVE

The next day Celeste kept Lucas home from day-care. They had breakfast with Filipe in his suite, then the three of them went for a walk at the beach. Lucas skipped ahead of them along the surf, while she and Filipe held hands and kissed along the way.

Everything looked different this morning. After such an emotionally charged day yesterday, today had dawned with brightness and hope, more hopeful and bright than she'd ever dreamed of having. She couldn't stop smiling.

After spending time on the beach, Celeste retrieved Senhor Xavier's notebook and gave it to Filipe. While he returned to the hotel to read it and meet with his manager, she and Lucas drove home to pack a bag with a change of clothes and some necessities. She had a feeling she and Lucas would be spending more and more time at the hotel in the coming days and weeks.

When they returned to the hotel, Filipe and Ross met them for lunch in the private lounge.

"Did you find what you needed?" she asked Filipe.

He nodded. "We did. Already met with my lawyer, and he gave me the green light to go ahead with the staff changes without any problems."

Ross ate quickly and stood. "If you'll excuse me, I have a staff meeting to set up and people to invite." He turned to Celeste with a conspiratorial look. "Just in case you're wondering, you're invited too. It starts at two."

She'd come to learn Ross Turner was Filipe's right-hand man, and she was glad he gave Filipe the support he needed to alleviate his responsibilities.

"Why do I have a feeling this will be a staff meeting for the history books?" she asked Filipe.

He chuckled. "That feeling is right. It'll be an historic meeting."

From the loaded looks between him and Ross, Celeste had a pretty good idea some big changes were forthcoming. Being invited to witness these changes only made her look forward to it even more.

Lucas had moved over to a printed rug where Filipe had set up a bucket of LEGO pieces for their mutual entertainment. She'd never tire of watching them play together.

Filipe walked over and sat on the rug. "Lucas," he said. "I got a message from Dr. Abarca. He said Flip should be good as new to return to his home tomorrow. What do you say we be there to welcome him back to the pond?"

"Yes, I want to be there," Lucas exclaimed, jumping up and down as he usually did to emphasize his words.

Celeste followed Filipe to the door and kissed him. "I'll see you later, then."

"I had another surprise for you, but after thinking about it, I better give you a heads-up." He returned the kiss and opened the door to leave, a decidedly playful expression on his face.

She tilted her head and raised her eyebrows. "A heads-up about what?"

"I don't want you getting annoyed at me for putting you on the spot in front of the rest of the staff." He let go of her hand and stepped into the hallway. "A promotion is coming your way."

"What promotion?"

She called after him, but he winked back as he got in the elevator, and the doors closed.

It could only be a promotion at the aquarium, but what did he mean specifically?

After the babysitter arrived to watch Lucas, Celeste walked down to the aquarium. She hadn't been there since Lucas's disappearance, not quite twenty-fours ago, but already it felt like so much longer. W

Ross met her just outside the main gates. "Hello, Celeste," he said with a smile. "Filipe sent me to escort you in, just in case. He's setting up for the meeting."

"Just in case Alice decides to block me?"

He chuckled. "Both Filipe and I believe in 'prepare and prevent' instead of 'repair and repent.'"

"How very true," she agreed, glad for the support. Even though Filipe was busy, he'd thought of her and had sent someone he trusted to watch out for her.

A long table had been brought to the staff lounge and chairs set around it. António Morais, Heitor, and Nuno Abarca were already sitting, and they greeted her sincerely.

"There you are," Filipe said when he saw her.

He stood to meet her and took her hand in a firm grasp. If they'd been at the hotel, she would have expected a warmer, more personal greeting. A kiss on the cheek, at least. But the aquarium was different, and she was relieved to see he understood that.

"I saved you a seat by me." Filipe led her to the chair at the front, on the right side of his at the head of the table. Ross took the seat opposite her. On the table, in front of Filipe, sat the black leather notebook that had belonged to Senhor Xavier.

Slowly the rest of the personnel came in, some smiling, some clearly looking forward to whatever Filipe would be announcing. When Alice arrived, she moved one of the chairs to the spot opposite Filipe, at the other end of the table. She looked around at the others but purposefully avoided Celeste.

"Welcome, everyone," Filipe started. "I appreciate you coming in today. We'll try to move quickly through the announcements so you can return to your duties and leave on time.

"As you know, the renovation crew is gone as a result of the inspection we had earlier this week. After careful consideration, and for personal reasons, I decided not to sell the aquarium."

A chorus of claps and approvals went around the room, and Filipe paused before continuing.

"As soon as we have new plans drafted, the renovation will resume in earnest, and we'll have a meeting then to show you those. To accommodate the expansion, new exhibits and animals will be brought in." He gestured to Nuno Abarca. "I'm pleased to announce Dr. Abarca as the new resident veterinarian and welcome him to the team."

Nuno smiled and waved. Celeste clapped along with the others, marveling at how much Filipe and Ross had accomplished this morning, barely containing the joy at all the forthcoming changes.

Filipe continued. "In the coming months, as the aquarium expands, we'll hire for new positions. Until then the staff remains the same—"

Alice rose from her seat. "Thank you, Senhor Filipe. As the SoliMar Aquarium's assistant director, I'll keep doing my j—"

"Excuse me," Filipe interrupted. "I'm not done."

Alice sat back down.

"As I was saying," Filipe went on, "the staff remains the same with the following exceptions: effective immediately, I'd like to welcome Celeste Ferreira as the new director."

He turned to her and smiled wide as the others clapped in approval. Celeste waved, her cheeks flaming at such enthusiastic approval and support. She'd have to thank Filipe later for the heads-up. It would have been very awkward for him to announce the new director without her knowing anything about it.

Everyone seemed pleased with the change. Except Alice.

She stood and splayed her hands on the table. "I fired Celeste yesterday. And now you make her the director? Do you know she never finished her degree? She's not qualified for the keeper position, let alone director."

"Sit down, Dona Alice," Filipe said firmly.

The room fell silent. Alice sat down, face scarlet. Celeste looked between Filipe and her, knowing his calm and confidence were those of someone who knew what he was doing.

He picked up the notebook and held it up. "The former director, António Xavier, kept meticulous notes about the aquarium, its workers, its animals, a little bit of everything really. I wasn't aware of it when I arrived, or I might have done things differently. Fortunately it came to light, and I'm now aware of several facts: first, you falsified your college records. Senhor Xavier investigated and found proof you were never enrolled in any university."

Alice moved to stand, but Ross had made it to her side and shook his head at her.

"Second," Filipe said, "you were habitually late to arrive and early to leave, and on several occasions you didn't clock in and out as you should. And third—well, I don't even need a third reason. Those two are enough. But knowing you purposefully harassed Celeste with your inexcusable behavior makes me glad I can personally guarantee you'll never work in this industry again. You're fired."

After staring down at Filipe for a long minute, Alice stepped away from the table.

Celeste held her breath, waiting for Alice to explode into a fit of rage, but the outburst didn't come. After everything that had happened—after everything Alice had done—it was strangely anticlimactic.

"Ross," Filipe said. "Please accompany Dona Alice to retrieve her personal effects, and make sure she exits the premises as soon as possible."

"My pleasure," Ross said, following closely behind.

As soon as they made it out the door, the staff erupted into loud cheers and clapping.

Celeste laughed, then covered her mouth. "It's not very professional, celebrating like this," she said to Filipe.

Filipe reached for Celeste's hand and pressed her fingers, smiling at her. "Who cares? You especially deserve to celebrate."

Her heart felt lighter already, what with her new position, the plans to reopen the aquarium, and, above all, Filipe's love for her and Lucas.

As everyone settled down and sat, Filipe turned to the staff. "I know things haven't been easy for a while, but I hope these announcements give you a glimpse of the changes coming and of the potential to turn the aquarium into a destination for families and ocean lovers that we can all be proud of. I believe together we can make it a successful venture.

"We'll have a proper staff meeting next week, but I wanted to add we'll be implementing a seven percent raise on all salaries, along with company health insurance, individual performance bonuses, vacation time, sick days and paid time off, and a retirement plan. Once the aquarium opens to the public, we'll add a quarterly bonus based on overall company performance and other benefits as we see fit. And that's all for today."

One by one, her colleagues approached to shake Filipe's hand. He spent a few minutes with each one, talking, laughing, and sharing stories.

When everyone was gone, Filipe took Celeste's hand and pulled her up from the chair. "Come here, beautiful," he said, wrapping an arm around her waist for a gentle hug.

She rested her hands on his chest and looked up at his warm brown eyes. "If I didn't know better, I'd think you're trying to impress me."

"Who says I'm not?" he asked in a teasing tone. "Did it work?"

"I'm thoroughly impressed, Filipe Romano," she replied. "I can't see how you'll be able to ever top yourself."

Filipe tightened his embrace around her, his gaze steady. "I think I'll be able to come up with a thing or two. Just wait and see."

Celeste chuckled. "You've ruined me for patience. I don't wait to wait."

But she would wait, and she'd enjoy the journey with Filipe by her side.

EPILOGUE

TWO MONTHS LATER

Filipe flexed his fingers, then quickly relaxed them as he realized he'd been doing the same all day. He slipped his hand in his jeans pocket, curling his fingers around the ring he'd picked for Celeste.

He took another deep breath. It was silly, in a way, all this nervous tension about proposing to her. He loved her. That wouldn't change. He loved Lucas as well and knew the boy reciprocated his affections. He even knew Celeste loved him—she'd said it to him plenty of times, in words, in kisses, in smiles and gestures he never wanted to forget.

There was nothing more right than the certainty of marrying Celeste and joining himself to her and her son. That he knew without a doubt.

The anxiety hiccupped inside him for the length of a flinch, then skittered away to make room for the conviction of their love. The nerves were only a kind of stage fright; nothing more.

When he arrived at the beach, Celeste and Lucas were already there, as they usually were on Monday mornings. The weekend guests at the hotel seldom lingered past Sunday night, and despite the calendar saying it was nearly the beginning of September, the weather felt more like early May—sunny, warm, with no signs of an impending change of season.

Lucas would start school one week from today, and Filipe wanted him to enjoy the last few days of summer vacation secure in the knowledge of their plans for the future.

The corner of Filipe's mouth hitched in a smile at what he'd planned for this moment. He'd involved Lucas, even though the little guy wasn't aware of Filipe's real intentions.

Filipe stood at the edge of the wooden walkway and looked around, contentment rising in his chest. Celeste and Lucas waved at him, and he waved back as they walked in his direction.

Just a few months ago he'd stood on this very spot feeling quite differently. The calm he'd felt back then didn't have the same completeness, not even an inkling of the happiness he carried today. He could hardly imagine more happiness after he married Celeste, but he also knew it would be there.

He turned to look at the hotel, another successful project, as he'd predicted. Surfing season would start in a few more weeks, and other than a few rooms they left open for special guests, they were booked out for the next eight weeks.

Peeking from behind the hotel, the lower building of the aquarium shone in the morning light. The license violations had been resolved, and the renovations had started in earnest to bring the aquarium to full activity, hopefully in the early spring, with new exhibits and tanks and lots of new animals. Much to Lucas's relief, the male swan had made a full recovery.

"Filipe," Lucas called out as he ran toward him. He stopped and took a couple of full breaths, then looked toward Celeste, who was still a few minutes from reaching them. "I did everything you asked for my mom's surprise."

Filipe bumped knuckles with Lucas. "Awesome. I sure appreciate your help, Lucas."

Lucas chuckled. "Mamã will be so surprised."

As long as she didn't freak out at what the surprise was and said yes.

Celeste reached them and slipped her arms around Filipe's middle. She leaned up for a kiss, and Filipe freely gave it, holding himself back from deepening the contact between them.

"You look mighty fine this morning," she said with a smile, a casual arm around his waist. "Like the king of the castle observing his kingdom."

"Do I?" He bent to brush another kiss. "Must be all this happiness I'm wearing. It looks good on me."

She chuckled. "And such modesty too."

"I don't need to be modest." He sobered as he pinned a steady gaze on her. "I know what I have and how lucky I am for it."

"Luck has nothing to do with it. You work harder than anyone I know. What you have, you deserve."

"I hope so," he replied.

Her eyebrows raised for a moment, as she didn't understand the full meaning of his words.

"Mamã," Lucas called. "Come see this." Lucas had walked off to a spot he and Filipe had prepared already. "You gotta come see this," he called again.

Celeste raised her arm and waved. "I'm coming." She turned to Filipe and took his hand. "Let's go see what he found this time."

Lucas had quite the collection of found objects he'd picked through summer, all kept in a shoe box he liked to call his treasure chest.

When Filipe and Celeste approached, a small corner of wood jutted up from the sand.

Lucas knelt beside it. "What do you think this is?"

Filipe suppressed a smile. The little guy was carrying out his role exactly as they'd rehearsed.

"Pull it out, Mamã."

"Why don't you pull it out? It'll be more fun for you to find out what it is."

He held up his palms. "My hands are tired from all the walking on the beach. You do it."

Celeste shook her head and laughed, then knelt beside Lucas. "I bet you won't be tired for dessert after dinner," she teased.

Lucas widened his stance. "I'll be all better for dessert." He winked with both eyes at Filipe over his mom's bent form, and Filipe winked back.

The exchange didn't go unnoticed, and Celeste frowned. "You two are up to something."

Filipe gestured at the small mound on the sand. "Aren't you going to pull it out?"

Celeste grabbed the exposed corner and pulled out a wooden frame with three heart stones in a close horizontal row, the middle rock smaller than the other two, and the one on the left larger than the one on the right.

She shook the sand off it, "Did you put this here?" she asked Lucas.

"No." His grin widened and Filipe grinned as well.

Celeste stood and read the caption, *We are family first in our hearts.* She looked between Lucas and him, her eyes already brimming with tears. "Did you make this?"

Lucas jumped up and down. "I helped Filipe find the stones," he declared enthusiastically. "Are you surprised?"

"Very much, Lucas."

As she turned her face to smile at Lucas, Filipe grabbed the ring from his pocket and dropped to one knee. "Celeste," he started, taking a deep breath as all the nervousness from before momentarily threatened to overcome him.

When Celeste found him down in front of her, she gasped and covered her mouth with her fingers.

"I fell in love with you when I was seventeen, and for years I dreamed you'd come to love me as well," he said to her. "I don't know what I've done to deserve having you back in my life, but I know I don't want to live without you and Lucas. I love you. I love both of you, and I want us to spend the rest of our days together." Another breath. "Celeste, will you be my wife?" he asked in a steadier voice.

Her eyes filled with fat tears, and she wiped at them as they rolled down her cheeks.

"Are those tears of happiness, Mamã?" Lucas chirped beside them.

Celeste extended her hand, a wide smile on her lips, and Filipe slipped the ring onto her finger. "Yes," she said firmly, her eyes never straying from Filipe's. "Yes, I will marry you, and yes, Lucas, these are tears of happiness."

BONUS CHAPTER

NINE MONTHS LATER

Celeste woke early and walked out onto the balcony in time to catch the sunlight as it rose from the east, behind the hotel.

For so many people, it was just a normal Saturday morning in early June.

For her and Filipe, it was their wedding day and it had finally arrived. She would become a Romano— Dona Celeste Romano, wife of Filipe Romano. Still a Quintano, but definitely not Ferreira anymore. A smile bloomed in her face.

The day dawned bright and clear, promising to be a warm one. The ceremony was scheduled to start just before sunset, with the reception and dance right after and into the night. Why hadn't they chosen to be married in the morning instead? Waiting almost all day would seriously challenge her patience.

At least she and Filipe had planned to have breakfast together with Lucas, despite the Romanos' insistence the groom couldn't see the bride on their wedding day or they'd surely bring bad luck on themselves. It would be the most covert, secret breakfast of her life. Luckily, no one else occupied the suites on the last floor, as she and Lucas had one for themselves and Filipe had the other one.

He had blocked out the SoliMar for their families and guests for the weekend, and some had already arrived last night. The rest would trickle in throughout the rest of the day. She and Filipe had set up rooms for visiting, games, and activities, and there was plenty to do to keep everyone entertained between the beach, the golf course, and the aquarium. Although she and Filipe would be leaving for the honeymoon sometime after the reception—or during, if Filipe had his way—everyone else was invited to stay until Sunday evening.

She walked back inside and checked in on Lucas. He still slept, askew on his bed, looking more like the little boy she still remembered than the big boy he proclaimed himself to be. Sleep relaxed and softened his features, and she resisted the urge to bend and kiss him on the forehead.

A soft knock sounded on the door, and she hurried to open it. Filipe slipped in, still wearing his pajama bottoms and a sleeveless shirt.

"Good morning, beautiful," he said, his morning voice husky and deep.

"Good morning, handsome," she said back to him.

He draped his arms around her back for a close embrace, and Celeste ran her hands on his upper arms, meeting him halfway for a languorous kiss.

Filipe reluctantly pulled away after a long moment. "Breakfast is coming in ten minutes."

"Lucas is still asleep," she said.

He brought her back into his arms with an arched eyebrow and a crooked smile on his lips. "Well, then. Let's make good use of this time, shall we?"

She went up on her tiptoes and wrapped her arms behind his neck as they resumed kissing.

When the kiss turned into something more, Filipe put some distance between them and sighed. "Is it too late to move up the ceremony to, say, in an hour?"

Celeste chuckled. "Like your family would let us."

"We could elope," he said with a hint of hope.

"Too late for that too," she said.

He took a deep breath. "Before Lucas gets up and breakfast gets here, I got something for you," Filipe said. He slipped a hand into the pocket of his pajama pants and drew out a slim box tied with a white satin ribbon.

"Filipe, you've given me so many gifts already," Celeste said. She took the pale-blue box and pulled at the bow.

"This one is special," he said in a low tone.

Inside, she found a bracelet made of gold links and charms. Filipe helped her clasp it around her left wrist.

"It has custom beads made of sea glass and sea-shells, all found on our beach walks together," Filipe said. "The seashells have been dipped in gold to make them more solid, and the charms represent important things and people in your life. The bracelet is one of a kind—like you."

A heart-shaped charm had the word *Mamã* engraved in the center; another one was a seahorse, which was the new logo for the aquarium, and the third was a pea pod with three peas inside.

"Remember how my grandmother had us shell peas on the back porch that summer when you and Eduardo came for a visit?" Filipe asked.

Celeste nodded, understanding the meaning of the charm.

She turned her wrist and the sea glass beads caught the light and reflected it back, and two golden shells dangled from the chain.

"This is so incredible," Celeste said, touching it. "You have put so much thought into this. How long have you been planning this amazing bracelet?"

He tilted his head and smiled softly. "Maybe since the day we became engaged?"

Celeste bracketed his face with her hands. "You are amazing, Filipe Romano." She went on her tiptoes and kissed him. "To know you've been planning this gift for that long—it touches my heart."

"Good. I did it right, then."

Celeste walked to the closet and slid its door open. "I was going to wait until we moved to the new house, but looks like this is the right moment for your gift." She picked up a framed rectangular print and held it up.

Filipe grabbed the other corner. "Is this the night sky?"

Celeste nodded. "It's a star map of a special night in Porto last year."

He read the date inscribed under the rounded representation of a dark night full of stars and planets. "It's the night we kissed."

A moment she wouldn't forget.

"It is," she said. "I was hoping you wouldn't remember it as the day your cousin Matias got married."

He placed the framed print on the floor against the wall. "No. It's our midnight kiss. This will go in our new home, in the bedroom," Filipe said.

In the house they'd been building for the past nine months, which would be ready to move into when they returned from their honeymoon to the Azores islands. A house overlooking the beach, not too far from the aquarium and the hotel. The home they would build together as a family, with Lucas.

"I'd like that," she said. "By the way, you have no idea how hard it was to find a meaningful gift for the man who has everything."

Filipe rested his hands on her waist. "I will have everything this evening, when we're officially married."

She couldn't agree more.

After a lively breakfast with a very excited six-year-old boy, Filipe left. They wouldn't see each other again until the ceremony. Not too long after, Filipe's mother fetched Lucas. Those two loved to spend time together.

Celeste walked to her bedroom, where her wedding dress hung from a padded hanger, and touched the fabric. Filipe had given her carte blanche with the budget, but that was not who she was. The only concession she'd made was to combine two different styles, the top of one and the skirt of another, into a custom-made dress that matched her personality, the venue, and the feeling of the reception.

Just a couple of shades warmer than white, in a flattering tone of light ivory, the softest tulle flowed into a skirt that brushed the floor. The form-fitting and sleeveless bodice in Chantilly lace added an elegant touch to an otherwise informal style. It was beautiful and completely fitting for a wedding by the beach.

Filipe's sister, Luciana, came to get her. "Are you ready to see the dining room? The hotel's team has done a spectacular job."

Gabriela, one of the Romano cousins, joined them. Filipe's immediate family and some of his cousins had taken their roles in the wedding seriously, and Gabriela was a sort of go-between for whatever need required attention.

When Celeste arrived downstairs, her jaw dropped in awe. The courtyard off the hotel's main dining room had been transformed with a white canopy decorated with hundreds of twinkle lights and garlands of realistic silk flowers. The aisle, coming off the main staircase and leading outside, had been flanked by rows of chairs in a quarter-moon pattern, and everything was dressed in a white background as the canvas for a palette of pastel colors. The effect was stunning in its understated beauty.

At the end of the aisle, on a half-moon dais decorated with yards of diaphanous material, Filipe would be waiting for her—she could almost see it all in her mind.

"It's beautiful," Celeste said. "They've done an amazing job."

Gabriela and Luciana agreed.

Off to the side, one of the wedding photographers took pictures of the decorations.

A team of three wedding photographers had been hired to record all the details for the day, one photographer each following Celeste and Filipe, and the this one here for the guests and decorations. Filipe had insisted on having more than one, saying one day they'd want to look back at everything that would make this day so magical and precious. In the end, it didn't take much on his part to convince her. She would want to remember every little thing of this special day—every moment, every word and every smile.

For a short while after they started their relationship, Celeste hadn't been aware of Filipe's net worth. He never flaunted his fortune, and he was generous in a practical way, preferring to help build structures and form jobs instead of handing out short-term solutions.

As Celeste became aware of her fiancé's wealth, she'd felt intimated at first, but under Filipe's guidance, she learned how to make a difference and was now in charge of a learning program about oceans and aquatic animals for school-aged children. She'd also re-enrolled in university and had only two more classes to finish before she could graduate.

For the wedding, instead of gifts, they'd both decided to ask their guests to donate to the clean water initiative Filipe had worked with in Angola, and with everyone's incredible generosity, they were on their way to providing enough funds for a new well and clean water education in a village that had neither. Filipe's world simply astounded her.

If they'd done this much even before getting married, how much more would they accomplish together when they became officially and legally united?

Celeste was so ready to start her life with Filipe.

The moment had finally arrived.

Filipe could hardly contain his excitement. After waiting all day—after waiting for nine months and a lifetime—he was about to enter the room where the ceremony was taking place.

The waning light, just before sunset, held the perfect blend of warm colors and radiant glow, illuminating the sand, the beach, and the blue waters beyond.

Instead of getting married in the church, he and Celeste had chosen to bring in an officiator and have the wedding at the hotel. The dining room had been transformed into a beautiful background worthy of the occasion.

Until then, Filipe stood in a small room off the dining room, waiting his turn to exit and walk out to the courtyard at the signal of Matias, his best man. Upstairs, on the first floor, Celeste was probably finishing her preparations to walk down the staircase and up the aisle toward him. He hadn't seen her since their stealth breakfast in the early morning, as they'd spent their day apart from each other and in the company of family and friends. As much fun as he'd had visiting with them, it was Celeste he wanted.

Anticipation was killing him.

A familiar face he hadn't seen in a long time appeared at the door.

"Sorry to drop by unannounced," the man said. "May I come in?"

Filipe smiled. "Damian Vaughn. What are you doing here?"

Damian entered the room and shook Filipe's hand. "Making myself late for a meeting in Lisbon, but I had to stop by and wish you well today."

"You're welcome to stay for the wedding party," Filipe teased.

"I wish I could. I only have a few minutes before my pilot calls me back. I wanted to personally invite you and your near-future wife to come stay at the island any time you want." Damian lived on a semi-private island in the Azores archipelago, where he owned a house that more resembled a hotel resort.

"That's very generous of you. Thanks, Damian."

A knock sounded at the door, and Gabriela poked her head in. "Filipe, Lucas wants to wait with you. Should I bring him down?"

"Yes, of course." He hadn't seen the little guy since that morning and missed him.

"Lucas?" Damian asked.

"Lucas is Celeste's son from her previous marriage, but I love him as if he were my own," Filipe replied, unable to keep the pride from his voice.

Damian stared at him, as if impressed. "To think a year ago we were working in Angola digging wells, up to our elbows in mud and plumbing parts. And now you're all domesticated, getting married and already doing the stepfather thing."

Filipe chuckled. "I heartily recommend domestication. It would do you well."

Damian shook his head. "Absolutely not. No wife and no kids for a long while. I'm doing fine on my own."

"Maybe you don't know what you're missing," Filipe said good-naturedly.

Just then the door opened wide, and Lucas entered the room. "Filipe, there's too many girls in Mamã's room. I want to wait with the men."

Filipe laughed at Lucas's serious expression and slightly annoyed voice, and Damian joined him.

"You can stay with me until cousin Gabriela calls you to stand in line," Filipe said. "How's that?"

"I'll come back for you later, Lucas," Gabriela said. She nodded at Filipe and then left.

The first bars of a popular song sounded suddenly, and Damian winced. "That is my cue. I'm afraid my time's up."

Filipe extended his hand. "I'm glad you stopped by."

"I apologize for my ill-timed appearance. Thanks for making the time to let me wish you well, and good luck with everything, especially married life," he added with a wink.

Filipe smiled wide. "I won't need any luck, but thanks." He was so ready for everything that came with the married life.

After Damian left, Filipe and Lucas played games until Matias returned.

"This is it," Matias said.

Gabriela appeared and took Lucas by the hand. "Come on, Lucas. Let's get you into the rest of your suit and in position for your mom."

The string quartet playing soft music shifted to the piece Filipe and Celeste had chosen to signal his entrance. Matias walked beside him to the front, where they stopped at the officiator's left.

Filipe took a deep breath.

The room was full on both sides, the happy faces of family and dear friends smiling with anticipation for the bride. As excited as everyone was, nobody could top his own eagerness.

When the music changed again, all in attendance rose from their seats and turned to the back of the room.

Filipe squared his shoulders and held his hands in front of him. It wasn't nerves he felt—only readiness and gratitude for everything that had led him and Celeste to his moment.

Her father walked her from the bottom of the staircase to the dining room, where the double doors had been opened wide. Lucas was there waiting for his mom and took her hand in his smaller one, then walked her to where the courtyard started. From there, Celeste made the rest of the way by herself.

Filipe kept a steadfast gaze on her, his eyes unable to see anything else. She looked more beautiful and serene than he'd ever seen her, in a gauzy dress with a lace top, with her hair halfway up with loose curls around her face and neck.

When Celeste finally reached him, Luciana took her bouquet, and Filipe held her hand, the hand of his future wife.

"I love you," he mouthed.

"I love you," she mouthed back.

As the ceremony started, it became a blur. Everything around him was only an impression, a hazy smudge in his peripheral vision—his focus completely fixated on Celeste.

When he finally heard the final words declaring them married followed by the invitation to kiss his bride, Filipe wound his arms around Celeste's waist and pulled her in for their first kiss as husband and wife.

Lucas was the first to clap and hoot, and everyone joined in, loud and crazy, laughing and cheering, as if it were the best thing to happen in a long time.

They were absolutely right, of course.

Celeste smiled against his lips. "We did it," she said, eyes sparkling.

He bent to kiss her again, not even trying to resist her gorgeous face and lovely mouth. "Yes, we did it. Here's to the rest of our lives together."

DEAR READER,

Thank you so much for reading Filipe and Celeste's story, *Kiss Me At Midnight*. I hope you've enjoyed reading it as much as I enjoyed writing it. You may learn more about them and their story on Pinterest.

Please consider leaving a review on Amazon and Goodreads. This is the best way to support me as an author.

For news of upcoming books and promotions, join my readers club.

I love to hear from readers! You can email me at lucinda@lucindawhitney.com.

Thank you!

Want to find out how Matias and Vanessa met? Turn the page to read *Meet Me at Sunrise*.

Read Matias and Vanessa's story
in *Meet Me at Sunrise*.

CHAPTER ONE

This was a bad idea. Why had she let Grandfather talk her into this trip?

Vanessa stopped at the entrance of the ship's formal dining room and gazed around. Outside the panoramic windows, the city of Porto inched up the hill from the docks on the other side of the river, the buildings and roofs and church towers competing for space unsuccessfully. Myriad lights shone against the night sky and spilled in reflective ribbons on the water's surface. In its architectural disorganization, there was a beauty that called to her. It was a city so unlike the ones she was used to. Much of Portugal was still a mystery to her.

Inside, the passengers sat in groups of eight at round tables, and waiters in white coats flitted between them with silver platters and bottles of wine. Everything in the room spoke of elegance and luxury, from the furniture and dark wood trim to the impeccably white tablecloths and fresh-cut flowers to the damask draperies drawn back with silver ropes and the pianist undulating at the baby grand.

She'd barely looked at the pamphlets Grandfather had sent her and was not prepared for the real-life opulence before her. She—the Kansas girl who preferred well-worn jeans and flip-flops to dresses and high heels—aboard the *MS Princess Catarina,* the crown jewel in Grandfather's fleet of luxury river ships. How long until someone recognized she didn't belong here?

A very bad idea indeed.

At least she was by herself. She'd managed to convince Grandfather she didn't need the bodyguard he'd planned to send with her. As president of a multi-million-dollar company, he was the one who needed bodyguards. She was just an American girl on her own, and nobody knew of her yet. Besides, what could possibly go wrong on a small cruise ship?

Inside her clutch, her phone rang. It was probably Dad. Again. He'd insisted on being able to contact her throughout the trip and had prearranged a new plan with Verizon. He'd have to wait until tomorrow to talk to her.

An appetizing scent reached her nose. Roasted pork, rosemary potatoes, and something else she couldn't identify. Vanessa was late to dinner and she had missed the "Welcome Aboard" cocktail party. The light breakfast from this morning was only a memory by now. Her stomach rumbled.

The maître d' appeared at her elbow. "May I have your name, please?"

Vanessa turned to him, grateful that English was the official language aboard. "Vanessa Clark. Is it open seating?" she asked, while he checked the list in front of him.

"Not for you, Miss Clark. Please follow me."

As he cut a path to the center of the dining room, Vanessa ignored the urge to smooth her dress and held on to her sequined clutch instead, carefully stepping on the gleaming wood floor and willing herself not to trip on her strappy sandals.

Was it her imagination or did most people pause to look at her? The conversations and clinking of silverware against the porcelain dishes continued on around them, as a few of the passengers darted their eyes at her. This was karma for being the last one to arrive at dinner. For someone who didn't like attention, she sure had a lot of it now.

The maître d' pulled out a chair next to a dark-haired man in a black uniform. He was clean-shaven and appeared to be in his early thirties, with an air of confidence that drew her attention. Who was he and what did he do?

The man stood and nodded at her. "Good evening, Miss Clark."

Her eyes widened for a moment. How did he know who she was?

He didn't smile openly, but his mouth curved into a pleasant expression, and Vanessa's lips rose in response.

"I'm glad you made it." His voice was deep and lightly accented, and his arresting brown eyes held hers for a moment longer than good manners called for.

After an awkward pause, they sat down and Vanessa dragged the bib-size napkin onto her lap, looking away from him and realizing the other guests at the table were staring at her. She drew a quick breath. There was a spotlight directly above, and the heat from it bore a hole in her head. Was the air conditioning even on? Goodness, he was just a man, and not even the most attractive one she'd ever met. Why the sudden discomfort?

"Is this your lovely wife, Captain?" The lady across from them asked.

Captain? Wife? Vanessa turned to the man, noting for the first time the white stripes on his sleeves. "I'm sorry, I didn't realize you were the captain." Her cheeks heated at the mistake. She was seated to the captain's right, without a doubt arranged by Grandfather.

He cleared his throat. "She is lovely but no, not my wife." He shrugged in a self-deprecating manner, and the other passengers at the table chuckled lightly.

He turned to her. "I'm Captain Romano, Miss Clark." He then addressed the other passengers who shared their table. "Allow me to introduce Miss Clark, from the United States of America." He started at his left and went around the table. "Dr. and Mrs. Whitehead, from the UK; Mr. and Mrs. Grantham, also from the UK; and Mr. and Mrs. Grosse, from Germany."

Vanessa nodded and smiled politely at them before they returned to their meals.

Miss Clark, I apologize for the blunder," one of the English ladies said. "But there was an empty chair next to the captain and he seemed to have been waiting for you." She looked between Vanessa and Captain Romano. "And you two make such a striking couple."

Vanessa's cheeks reddened, the curse of a light complexion, courtesy of Dad's Scandinavian ancestry.

"I haven't had the pleasure of meeting Miss Clark until now," the captain said.

Vanessa nodded. "Yes, what he said." She cringed inside. Why couldn't she come up with an appropriate reply when she needed one?

She busied herself with the perfectly seasoned potatoes on her plate instead. If she nodded and looked interested in the conversations around her, maybe she wouldn't have to say too much and could save herself from any more embarrassing responses.

"What state are you from, Miss Clark?" the German man asked, his accent evidence of his origins.

Vanessa paused to look at him. "I'm from Kansas."

His forehead wrinkled and he looked at his wife who gave him a small shrug.

"It's in the middle of the country. You know, lots of farming and fields, *The Wizard of Oz* and tornadoes," she explained, her words running together.

They nodded in understanding. Maybe she should stop talking now.

Vanessa waited for more questions, but thankfully none came, and she slowly let out a small breath of relief as the attention shifted from her.

One of the English men put his fork down. "Captain Romano, is Chef Teresa still on your crew?"

The captain smiled. "She certainly is. In fact, I have the same exact crew as last year." The pride in his voice was unmistakable.

Was this a common occurrence, to ask after the crew? Her knowledge of cruise etiquette was ridiculously poor despite what she'd read before coming, and even though Grandfather owned the vessel.

The questions continued for the rest of the meal, keeping the captain busy as he gave everyone his attention. How did he find the time to eat? His patience was admirable.

As the courses changed, the captain picked up the bottle of red wine, and Vanessa watched him pour a glass of the burgundy liquid for her. She thanked him and brought the glass to her lips, tasting a drop too small to swallow. The flavor was foreign to her, and she chased it down with a large gulp of the mineral water from the other tall glass in front of her. As she set the glass down, her hand trembled, and she tightened her grip on the stem until the base touched the table. How much longer until she could take refuge in her cabin?

As another waiter slipped a plate with the next course in front of her, she looked casually to the neighboring tables.

Couples. All the passengers sitting in the dining room were couples. Middle-aged and senior couples eating and talking and laughing. She couldn't find another person close to her age among the hundred and thirty passengers. The growing uneasiness tightened in her chest, and she suppressed a sigh. What had Grandfather done, sticking her on a fancy river cruise with the upper crust of Europe?

Captain Romano leaned in her direction. "Is everything all right, Miss Clark?"

Vanessa's tongue stuck to her palate, and she took another drink of the barely cold water. "Please, call me Vanessa, Captain." She raised her eyes to him. "Have you met my grandfather?"

One of the waiters came to the captain and handed him a small card. He tucked it in his pocket and then turned to the rest of the table. "Excuse me, ladies and gentlemen. I am needed elsewhere for a moment."

As he stood, he made eye contact with Vanessa. "Excuse me, Miss Clark," he said to her.

Vanessa nodded in response, not knowing what else to say. Why did he single her out?

What an unfortunate time for him to leave, and how disappointing for her. Now she'd have to wait for another chance to ask him about Grandfather.

Matias Romano looked around for the cruise director. When he spotted her across the room chatting
with a group of passengers, he rose and excused himself from the last table. He always took the time to
greet all the passengers after dinner and he wouldn't
start making exceptions on this trip. But he could
leave the rest of the evening in Anabela Rialto's
capable hands. Mingling and interacting with the
passengers were some of her duties, and Matias had
observed over the last few trips and she seemed to
enjoy that part of her job.

He had other matters to think about. Like Miss
Vanessa Clark. They hadn't had a chance to talk
in private at the table, and she had left the dining
room abruptly after the dessert course was cleared,
not even waiting for the after-dinner espresso to be
served. If she had returned to her cabin, he'd have to
talk to her some other time. But leaving her question
unanswered wasn't ideal, and he felt obligated to set
a friendly tone between them.

He quickly exited through the main lobby and
climbed the stairs to the sun deck. He stopped short
before reaching the bridge. There she was, to the
starboard side, leaning casually by the railing, looking out to the city on the other side of the river. Her
face was in profile, and her long blonde hair blew
gently in the breeze. It was a lovely scene and she
was a lovely woman, but there was nothing more to it.

So what if he was partial to blondes? A pretty face didn't hold much interest for him when she'd behaved so snobbishly at dinner. She had picked at her food and barely spoken to any of the other passengers, gazing around the room with an air of aloofness instead. As the only granddaughter of the company's president, she was probably used to the royal treatment, but that didn't give her the right to look down on the other passengers. Suddenly, talking to her wasn't a pressing matter anymore.

Why had he agreed to António Valadares's harebrained idea? Sure, he could hardly deny any request from the president of the entire fleet of river cruise ships, but acting as a personal guide to his heiress granddaughter was not in Matias's job description. He should have said no, plain and simple. He was the captain, not a babysitter to a young woman who had everything. But his sense of duty had prevailed instead, as it usually did. There was more at stake than his personal preferences. Senhor Valadares had hinted at a problem with the future of the company, but Matias wasn't sure how it tied to the granddaughter.

Matias slowed down and squared his shoulders, letting out a slow breath. A hint of anticipation flared up, and he quickly squelched it, annoyed with himself at the twinge of attraction that sparked for a second too long. He only needed to talk to her. Nothing more.

She stood barefoot, her high-heeled sandals lying on their sides, her small purse next to them. Matias resisted the urge to return them to her and shoved his hands in his pants' pockets. He cleared his throat to greet her, but she spoke first.

"How many times have you made this trip, Captain?"

"Quite a few, Miss Clark." He faced the city as she did.

This was his seventeenth time up the river on this particular route. He knew because he'd been recording all his trips—not only the cruises but also the fishing and stocking ones—since he'd boarded his first boat as a deck hand at the age of fourteen. There were official records as well but he didn't like admitting to that level of precision and mostly kept the exact number to himself. "Miss Clark—"

She interrupted him. "And just how long have you been working for this company?"

Matias turned to her. "Is there a reason to your questioning, Miss Clark?" He kept his tone level and even, but his fingers tightened around the key ring inside his right pocket. What was it about this woman? He'd barely met her, and already she set him on edge in a way no one else had in his recent memory.

She leaned away from the railing and turned partially to him. "Just trying to determine how well you know my grandfather."

"Yes, you asked me that earlier. I'm sorry I didn't reply." They'd been interrupted by another passenger needing help, as he was so often during meals.

Matias took a quick breath and braced himself for more questions. He didn't know what to expect from her and it made him uneasy. The reaction was new to him, but she was more than a simple passenger, and it would serve him well not to forget the connections she had. "I have met your grandfather on several occasions since I started working at the company."

She turned away from him and let out a long sigh. "Probably more times than I have." Her words came out quick and low, and maybe not intended for him to hear.

"Is there a problem?" He paused and made eye contact.

"Not a problem exactly." She looked away and drummed her fingers along the rail.

"Is there something you're not happy with, Miss Clark?" They hadn't even departed, and already she had complaints. Usually he left the passenger-related matters to his cruise director, but not this one. She was in his hands, whether he liked it or not. "I know you're probably used to more personal service, but if you give us a chance, you might be pleasantly surprised."

Miss Clark's eyebrows knit in a scowl, but she didn't comment right away. After a long moment, she asked, "Are all the cabins as large as mine?"

"Excuse me?"

"The cabin assigned to me. Is that the standard cabin size?" She fidgeted with a length of hair, and when his eyes turned to it, she dropped it and flicked it behind her back.

The gesture lasted only a few seconds, but he lost his train of thought as it latched onto the woman in front of him. Matias struggled to resume their strange conversation. "Actually," he shook his head. "Uh, no. Your cabin is one of two deluxe cabins on the ship. We refer to them as the grand cabins, and they're reserved for our VIP passengers."

It was her turn to shake her head. "He did it, didn't he? He put me in that cabin?"

This conversation was turning more bizarre each minute. "If there's a problem with your cabin, I'll ask Miss Rialto to look into it. She's our cruise director, and I'll introduce you if you haven't had the chance to meet her. Your grandfather requested you stay in that particular cabin since it's the largest and best on the ship, and I have an obligation—"

Her eyes went wide. "Obligation? Obligation to what?"

Not to what, to whom. Her, to be exact. Matias didn't reply.

"To me, isn't it? You were going to say you have an obligation to me, weren't you?"

Matias flinched at her words and the way she'd read his mind. He rubbed his forehead. "It's not like how you make it sound." He forced his eyes to her. "Yes, I have an obligation toward you but it's the obligation I have toward all the passengers on board as well as my crew. I am the captain, after all."

Her shoulders relaxed a fraction, and Matias pressed on. "Your grandfather only wanted to make sure you have the best experience on this trip and even you can't fault him for that." Matias knew from his own research that she was his only granddaughter.

"I'm sure he did." She shook her head lightly, and her shoulders slumped even more, as if something weighed on her. "I don't need a babysitter, Captain. In case you haven't noticed, I'm a grown woman."

He'd noticed all right. More than he wished to, but he wouldn't be telling her that.

"Did he tell you why he wanted me to take this trip?" she asked.

Matias fumbled to find a reply and she waved him off. "That's okay, I don't want to know what he said. There's enough drama as it is."

It was family drama and he should stay out it. Well, most of it. He was already involved.

After a moment, she straightened and met his eyes. "At what time does the boat leave tomorrow?"

"The ship departs after lunch." He emphasized the word to correct her. It certainly wasn't a boat. "There's a guided excursion in the morning."

She bent to pick up her shoes and tucked the purse under her arm. "What are the rules about leaving?"

"Any time the ship is docked, you can leave at your leisure. But if you don't make it back before departure, we can't hold it for you."

She nodded. "That's only fair."

As she walked past him, he cleared his throat. "Nobody will prevent you from leaving if that's what you wish to do, but I hope you'll consider staying, Miss Clark." He wanted her to stay, and not just because the company's president had asked him. Proving to her that the trip was one worth taking had become more important than he'd anticipated.

Before she reached the staircase, he called after her. "Miss Clark."

She stopped and looked over her shoulder.

"Please be careful when you come out on the sun deck." He looked down at her bare feet, and she followed his gaze. "Oftentimes the floor is wet and it's easy to slip. I wouldn't want you to get hurt."

She pivoted, raising her fingers in a mock salute. "Aye, aye, Captain."

Find *Meet Me At Sunrise* on Amazon

THE AUTHOR

$\mathcal{L}$ucinda Whitney was born and raised in Portugal, where she received a Master's degree from the University of Minho in Braga, in Portuguese/English teaching.

She lives in northern Utah with her husband and four children. When she's not reading and writing, she can be found with a pair of knitting needles, or tending her herb garden.

She's the author of *Romano Family* series, of which Kiss Me At Midnight is the fifth book. She also authored *The Secret Life of Daydreams* and *One Small Chance*.

Please visit her website at lucindawhitney.com for more information and news.